ELM CITY BLUES

A TOMMY SHORE MYSTERY

LAWRENCE DORFMAN

ROUGH
EDGES
PRESS

ELM CITY BLUES

PART 1

ONE

I was sitting at my usual half booth at the Anchor when I saw her enter. It was a little before one o'clock on a Friday, too early for a good cup of coffee and a cigar next door at the Owl Shop. She'd come through the door quickly and stopped about 6 feet in, as if still trying to convince herself that what she was doing was worth being in a place like this. Looking around, she spotted me and walked over.

"Thomas Shore?"

I smiled at the use of my full name. Most people called me Tommy and a few close friends called me T. Only my ex-wife and my late mother called me Thomas. And only when I was in trouble. Which was pretty much all the time.

"That would be me. What can I do for you?"

She looked around furtively, with a look on her face like she smelled something that was slightly off.

"May I sit down?"

The half booths at the Anchor were vinyl, plastic faux leather, and had been installed sometime in the late 40's. There were three of them and mine was farthest from the door. They were all badly worn, with various rips and tears. This one was in the best shape of the three.

I ate lunch here almost every day. The food was bad but they gave you a lot. I could read the New York Post, sip a ginger ale, and eat a burger or a BLT. On Friday's they made pot roast sandwiches but you had to get here early. They were only $2.50 and came with fries. If you got here much past noon, you had to stare down one of the homeless guys who worked the block to get enough quarters to eat there. They served me so clearly they served everybody.

I slid over and motioned for her to sit. And even though she had asked me if she could, I could see she was having second thoughts.

"I just ate so I don't bite," I said. Mr. Charm School.

It may have been my imagination but I could swear I heard her "harrumph", like in an old Myrna Loy movie. I chuckled a little.

She shot me a look. "You find me funny?' She was trying hard to keep the upper hand but was losing that battle quickly.

About 45, she was well-kempt and impeccably groomed. Everything in place and a place for everything. She carried an expensive Bottega Veneta bag, a black leather shoulder deal. Probably ran two Grand. She put that on the seat beside her, her left hand resting on it.

She was wearing a stylish two-piece suit, short jacket and mid-calf skirt. Tweed or one of those fabric-y types. Expensive but Nordstrom expensive, not Neiman-Marcus expensive.

She was also wearing black six-inch heels. My ex-wife had been a piece of work but the one thing she had taught me that actually stuck was that you could tell almost everything you wanted to know about a woman by her shoes. These shoes said money.

"Do you have a name?"

She glared. "Of course, I have a name." She smiled a little when she caught on that I was teasing.

"Miriam Ross." She held out her hand in a way where I was unsure whether she expected me to kiss it or shake it. I took the fingertips and shook them a little. Not pleasant.

It was an old-fashioned name; one you would associate with someone from the past that held an old-fashioned job. Seamstress or switchboard operator. She was immaculate so I immediately ruled out chimney sweep.

"Nice to meet you. What can I do for you?"

"I understand you're a jack-of-all-trades, yes? That you do private investigations, yes?"

"Yep, everything but plumbing."

Again, that confusing look on her face. She wasn't used to talking to the help.

"You fancy yourself as amusing, yes?"

The thing she did with the questions at the end of every sentence was starting to annoy me but I stayed civil. I was pretty sure I could take her if it came to fisticuffs. And it had been a while between pay days.

"Well, I'm no Richard Pryor but I crack myself up from time to time." I was getting bored on top of it.

"Well, I want to hire you."

I was no longer bored.

I sat back and looked at her again, weighing how much compensation to ask for. I was going to go all out.

"I get $250 a day plus expenses. Three day minimum." I was unlicensed so I tried to keep the money reasonable. I didn't need the State of Connecticut aware of me. At that price, if someone was "unsatisfied", they'd write it off as you get what you pay for. Asking for more could be a problem.

"Do you take cash?" she asked, already taking an overstuffed envelope out of her tony purse. She had been willing to pay more. Damn.

She slid 10 crisp $100 bills over to me. I looked around out of habit and pocketed them quickly.

"Just make those?" Definitely not Richard Pryor.

She ignored that and settled in to tell me her story.

"Can I get a drink, please?"

I put up two fingers to get the barmaid's attention. Sally was somewhere between 85 and 150 years old. She'd been at the Anchor since the end of WWII.

It worked as well as it always did. She ignored me.

"What would you like?" I asked, getting up to go to the bar. I found myself wondering if they had sarsaparilla.

"Scotch, neat. And a Diet Coke on the side."

I squinted a little but let it go. I expected the diet soda. The booze was a surprise this early. Oh well, takes all kinds.

When I returned with the drinks, she was looking into the mirror of a small compact, applying a fresh coat of lipstick.

"Expecting company?"

She glanced my way quickly but kept on painting.

"A girl can never be too glamorous, you know... if

you let the little things go, everything else is sure to follow." She looked me up and down so fast you needed to be looking hard to see it, but it was there.

I looked down at what I was wearing. A classic Joseph Abboud blue blazer, crisp white shirt (well, not so crisp), and jeans. And Timberlands. Because I liked them. Comfortable. I realized I was a little too old for that look but hey, no one was hiring me for my fashion sense.

She finished up, snapped the compact shut, tossed it into her bag and prepared to drink. "Ahhh..." she sighed, like it was the first of many to be had that day. I sipped my ginger ale. "Shall we get down to it?"

"I'm all ears."

TWO

"I need you to find my son, David."

I was struck by the lack of any emotion in her voice as she said it. My gut feeling about her was that emotion wasn't something that came easy.

"Okay. How old is he and when did you last see him?"

She paused. She had clearly rehearsed this scenario in her mind before coming in here but it wasn't going the way she planned.

"It's been a week. He turned 22 a week ago and lives with me now that his father's gone. He's usually home every night, sometimes late, but he always comes home. He likes to sleep late in the morning, then goes to his job at Donut Crazy on York Street. Sometimes he'll go out afterwards but he always comes home. He hasn't in a week."

"Did you report it to the police?"

She looked away. "Not yet. I think he's gotten into something bad and I don't want to involve the authorities yet."

A number of questions went through my head. Why wait a week to report it? What kind of bad things? What happened to the dad? Did they still have those Maple Bacon donuts at Donut Crazy?

I took out a pen and the little pad I stole off the desk at the Omni hotel.

"What kind of bad things?"

She was playing with the napkin that had been under her drink, fraying it into little pieces.

"I found some stuff in his room when I was cleaning. Tubes and bottles and the like. There was a horrible aroma coming off everything."

I looked at her, trying to assess whether she was naïve and innocent or just stupid.

"Has he had problems with substance abuse before, pot or booze or anything like that?"

"No, never," she said, too quickly.

I'd get back to that. "What did it smell like?"

She blushed a little. "Well, we don't have a cat but there was a vague odor like cat urine... or rotten eggs. Definitely sulfurous...old garbage."

"Huh," I'd grunted. She could be describing my apartment on certain days but my first thought went to meth.

"Anything else?"

"Maybe ammonia?"

Definitely meth.

"Does David have a girlfriend?"

She pursed her lips. "He's been seeing this one girl recently. I'm not really happy about it. She's comes over late sometimes. We've never really been properly introduced. Very thin. Too thin. Melissa or Marissa, something like that. I have no idea what her last name could be." She looked like she would be dismissive of any girl David brought home that wasn't Princess Di.

"Do you know if they hung out anywhere special? Did he mention any clubs or bars or places they liked to go?"

She looked down and pretended to think.

"Well, I seem to recall a place called Diesel Lounge. Is that a club?"

She knew the answer but I played along.

"It is. Down on State Street. Mixed bag of people go there. Gets wild sometimes."

"Well, that was the one I believe he mentioned going to... usually on his way out the door. We used to have a great relationship...he always told me everything. But after his father passed, he closed down. Starting staying out late, seeing this girl. His temper changed, too. He snapped at me a lot. For nothing! If I asked him even one question..."

This could have gone on for a while so I interrupted. "Okay, so you've paid me for four days. I'll ask around, see what I can find out, see if anyone's seen him and will let you know. Do you have a cell?"

She pulled it out of her bottomless bag. It was the latest iPhone X.

"I can never remember it. Here it is. 203-656-2992. I'll leave it on." She held it up to her face to log on. Good thing David wasn't trying to call her before now.

"Great. Here's my card. I'll give you a call sometime tomorrow." I wanted to know more. I wanted to find out how her husband died and where she lived and the rest of the story but that was for another time. Right now I wanted a smoke and a coffee and to get in touch with one of my guys.

"Okay then." She rose quickly, like an unpleasant task had been completed.

I ate a few fries and paid the check. It took a while for Sally to find change for a crisp, new hundred-dollar bill.

THREE

I needed three things. I needed to think, I needed a good cup of Joe, and I really needed a great cigar so I did what I usually did at that time; I went next door to the Owl Shop.

The Owl Shop had been in New Haven since 1929. Started as a cigar store, the owner's son added a bar just before the smoking laws changed and it was the only bar in Connecticut you could smoke and drink in. At night it could get pretty crazy, a mix of different crowds from different parts of the city, but during the day it was usually quiet.

Bill, the day manager, was standing behind the first glass counter, smoking a cigar and looking at some paperwork. It wasn't the first stogie he'd had that day. It was barely 1:30.

"What's shakin', William? Life treating you good?"

He looked up briefly from his order forms, saw it was me, then went back to ordering more cigars. It was his favorite thing to do, after smoking and drinking and golf.

"Same old shit, new day. It was crazy busy in here."

I looked around. There was an old guy asleep in one of the leather chairs in the back and Callie, the bartender, mindlessly wiping down the bar and watching "Wheel of Fortune" on the TV over the bar. And me. No one else.

"I can see where you might have had to beat 'em off with a bat."

"Not now, wiseass, before...we sold a ton of cigars."

I nodded. Best not to engage.

"Hey, has Reilly been in yet?"

"Haven't seen him. I was in back for a while, though."

There was a walk-in humidor in the back of the place. Bill took inventory there every day. It had a glass wall that separated it from the rest of the bar so anyone working in there could keep their eye on what was happening in the bar. If they were so inclined. Bill usually wasn't.

"Well, if he comes in, tell him I'm looking for him. We got a gig."

"Some widow needs you to recover her dead husband's pension?" He chortled at his little joke.

Don't engage. Don't engage.

"Yeah, something like that. Tell him, okay?"

"Whatever."

Jeez. It was like someone had a sale on beds that came with two wrong sides and the entire city of New Haven bought one.

"Thanks. I'll be in my office."

He chortled again and waved me off.

Reilly was a lanky Irishman that I used for leg work. About 6'4, he liked to wear leather trench coats, ripped jeans, beat up Doc Martins and changed off between a Clash T-shirt, a Ramones sweatshirt and a CBGB hoodie. He was 53 years old.

I'd met him in the Owl 10 years before, when he lived across the street from the bar in the Taft Hotel. The Taft was a holdover from the glory days when New Haven was a bedroom city to New York. Converted to apartments in the 60s, they maintained a doorman who slept most of the time and most of the rooms were rented by artists or Yale students. He was the former. He would know where the meth crowd hung out.

I sat at the one chair facing the door at the end of the bar. It had been my ex's favorite place to sit, where she could hold court with her friends. Since the divorce, she rarely came into the joint.

Callie set me up with a double Americano as I unwrapped a Davidoff Nicaraguan, robusto sized.

Just enough to get me relaxed and ready to start finding David.

The cigar was nearly perfect. Burned slowly and had great taste. I was so into it I barely heard Simone come up behind me.

Simone was a head case. The Owl staff tolerated her because she drank a lot and paid her bill monthly. Trust fund thing. At one time, she probably tested genius, but booze and cigarettes and stress and life took its toll on her and she was now a few steps shy of bag lady status. I put her age somewhere between 40 and 80, leaning hard towards the latter. I hadn't even seen her come through the door.

"Hey, can I get a light off that?" She pointed at my cigar lighter.

"Sure. But be careful. You can weld with this thing." I handed it to her and watched closely.

She laughed. "Yeah, maybe burn the city down, huh? That would be something, huh?"

I looked at her fully and saw that she was not close to being near planet Earth. Best to just agree.

"Whatever you say, Simone." She was having trouble so I grabbed the lighter from her and lit her cigarette. She had a nearly full pack of American Spirits but they would go quickly.

"What's the what?" she asked.

The last thing I needed or wanted was this conversation so I said, maybe a little too brusquely, "Working a case, Simone. Can't chat."

I glanced over at her and saw that I'd hurt her feelings. But if I said anything else, it would be like opening a door. She moved away to one of the high-top tables, muttering to herself.

I sat there for a half hour more, sipping my Americano, smoking the cigar and running over the conversation from an hour ago. Something wasn't sitting right but I couldn't put my finger on it.

I called Reilly the Irishman and left a message on his phone. He ran a fairly successful property inspection business when he wasn't painting or drinking or getting high. He was probably busy. I relayed a few details and asked him to call me.

I decided that I needed to get started. I paid my tab and walked out the front door. I saluted Bill.

He didn't look up.

Walking over to the Taft, I paused to look up at the front of the building. I was always taken aback by the grandeur of the place. It used to be a truly great hotel back when New Haven was a thriving town.

I was living there now, using the front room of my place as an office. It helped to cut down on the overhead.

I had a first floor, two-bedroom apartment. 1C. Not a lot of windows but the ones I did have looked out on the alley that ran down to Temple Street. It was great most of the time except on St. Patrick's Day parade day, when the alley doubled as a bathroom. Still, I liked living there.

As I entered from the lobby, one half of the lesbian artist couple who lived next door was in the hallway leading to my apartment. She was applying enamel paint to an old bike. She'd laid down a small tarp but paint was still going everywhere.

"Chloe. Working hard, eh? Making a bit of a mess, no?"

She looked up, surprised. "You're not here?"

Not feeling overly metaphysical, I laughed. "Oh, but I am here."

She furrowed her brow. "No, I mean you're not there. In your apartment. I thought I heard you banging around in there."

I glanced over to the door and could see it was unlocked and not quite closed. I reached in my pocket and pulled out the sap I carried. It was an illegal weapon and I would get hassled if caught with it by the cops but I had never been too keen on guns or knives. This little baby fit in the side pocket of my sports coat and was quick and easy. I never had to use it but it gave me comfort carrying it.

I asked Chloe to go into her apartment and lock the

door. She huffed about it a little but glanced at the blackjack and then went inside her place. I opened the door to my place slowly.

The door to the fridge was open and all I could see was the ass of a pair of black jeans and a torn leather jacket. The big Irishman looked up from his rummaging, smiled and said, "Hola! Nothing much in here to eat, Hoss!"

FOUR

I tried to compose myself but my heart was racing. It took a second for it to get back to normal.

"Jeez, Reilly, you scared me half to death. I thought you were some punk that was robbing me. How'd the hell did you get in?"

I threw the sap on the little table near the door.

Reilly chuckled. "I still got a key. This used to be my apartment, remember, Sherlock? Scared... what are ya, losin' it? How about growing a pair?"

He always did have a knack for making you feel both confident and positive about yourself.

"I'm not 'losing it', I just wasn't expecting anyone to be here." I wanted to change the subject quickly. "Hey, I left you a message. Did you get it?"

"Yeah, already on it. I was at Christy's watching the Liverpool game when you called. Game was tied so I didn't answer, but when I heard the message, I asked Tony, the guy who works the bar there, if he'd heard of David Ross. He said no, but he knew a guy that died a year or so ago, named James Ross and said that that he might have had a son name David. Got a pic of the kid?"

Reilly was talking a mile a minute, probably the result of the three or four Jameson's he usually had while watching a soccer match. Sometimes mixed with a valium or two. He had been dealing with some health issues recently. I silently kicked myself for not asking for a picture. Probably too focused on the 10 new Benjamins.

"No, but I'll get one. I can google her now, though, and maybe there's a picture of him there, and maybe something on the dad."

He had a disgusted look on his face. "Man, you never ask enough questions. Maybe you should send away for that "Learn to Be a PI at Home" kit they advertise in the magazines?"

It was like this every time. I got to pay him out of my cut and he got to give me a huge ration of shit in exchange. He thought it was a good deal. I was on the fence.

I opened the old laptop I was able to keep from the divorce and waited for it to boot up. It had been my father's when he and my mother had their antique business that they used to keep track of sales and inventory. That was over 15 years ago.

Rina, my ex, got all the good stuff we'd bought in the 10 years we were together. Including the Mac, the Audi, the house (which she sold), the stocks, the timeshare in Newport (which I hated), the 52-inch LG television (which she hated)... and pretty much everything else of value. Rina was short for Irina and she was of Russian descent – part Bolshevik, part Trotskyite and part Russian Wolf hound. We were still friends but there were absolutely no benefits.

The laptop finally started up and I googled Miriam Ross.

There wasn't much there. A high school prom picture posted on her Facebook page. Her wedding announcement. A few odd pieces on some community projects she was involved in.

The surprise came from two articles in the New Haven Register about her husband, James.

The first was an announcement of bankruptcy. He had evidently been running a successful real estate business but something had happened and he had lost it all.

The second was his obituary. He had died in a fire at one of the properties that he was having trouble selling. What was left of his assets had gone to Miriam and son David. The business went to his partner, Jack Callen.

"This is interesting."

Reilly came up behind me and looked over my shoulder at the small screen. He'd made a sandwich out of the last of the French Ham and Brie I'd just bought and was chomping on it noisily.

"Huh. Arson? That puts a bit of a different spin on things."

I looked at him. "I'm not going to go there yet, but we should get into it a little more. You know that guy at City Hall, the guy we got the Steve Earle tickets for? Sean? Maybe he can get the records on some of these buildings the husband owned. She looks and dresses like money but this says they lost it all. Purse alone was maybe 2 Grand. And the real deal too, not a knockoff."

Reilly looked at me. "What are you, an expert on accessories now? Jeez. Maybe you should change jobs and become a fashion consultant?"

I decided to take the same tack with him that I took with Bill at the Owl. I didn't engage. He went back to look in the fridge again, having finished the sandwich. It must have been a disappointment because he slammed the door, said "Oi, fuckin' Oi! Off like a prom gown!" and left, saying he would hit me up later if he found out anything.

I took a moment and basked in the silence. I looked around the Internet a little more. There wasn't much there and absolutely nothing on David Ross. I was getting a little frustrated until I remembered Miriam had mentioned a girlfriend, either Marissa or Melissa, and that they hung at Diesel. Maybe she worked there? I googled it and their Facebook page came right up. Along with a picture of one of the bartenders making a drink. One Marissa Grant. Bingo.

Diesel was a 15-minute walk from my apartment and I flip-flopped on whether to call an Uber. On the other hand, Shake Shack was on the way and it was getting near dinner time. I opted to walk. A couple of Smokestack burgers and a coffee shake and I would be ready to start sleuthing again.

FIVE

It was still chilly out so I walked at a fairly brisk pace. April can go either way here but the winter had been harsh and we were only a few days into the month. I had changed into a hoodie and was wearing an insulated Columbia jacket but I still felt the cold. Perhaps a detour to the Trinity Bar for a quick shot or two of Jameson before I got to Diesel would help.

I veered off onto Orange Street from Chapel. Trinity had just recently opened after a fire had gutted the place last fall. It was heartbreaking for the regulars, of which both Reilly and I counted ourselves among.

They served a terrific egg sandwich for breakfast that went perfectly with the best Bloody Mary in the city. Nothing fancy, just delicious - a good tomato juice, a few shots of lemon juice, a few shots of lime juice, some pickle juice, pepper and fresh horseradish. On hangover days, a shot of Tabasco. They carried all the soccer games around the world and the bar would be full at 8 in the morning. It got a little raucous sometimes but was always great fun. It had been touch and go whether they'd reopen but they crowd-shared enough money to make up for the insurance shortfall and had been open for 3 weeks.

I walked in and went to the left bar. There were booths on the right for diners but, aside from breakfast, they weren't really a food destination. There was a lingering smell of smoke in the air and I thought they may not ever get rid of that. Shane, the owner and bartender, set me up immediately with a shot of Jamo without my having to ask.

"Thank you, kind sir!" I tended to slip into a makeshift brogue when I went in the place. Shane, born and bred in Dublin, tolerated it for the most part.

"What are you up to, Tommy?" I loved the way he said my name. Reminded me of the Clancy brothers we used to watch on the Ed Sullivan show.

"Not a lot. Got a gig. Lady wants her kid found... well, he's not really a kid, the guy is in his twenties but he lives at home and hasn't been there for a week. Paid me cash so I'm flush." Always good to put Shane's mind at ease from the jump.

"That right? Well, kids these days, eh?" I nodded. It was the kind of bar where no cliché went unspoken.

"His old man died a few years back, guy name of James Ross. You didn't know him, did ya? Ever see him in here? He was some kind of real estate mogul until his biz went belly up. "

Shane's face had gone even more pale than usual. He stared at me for a few seconds longer than I would have expected and said, "Yeah, I knew that son of a bitch."

I nearly spit up my drink. It had been a shot in the dark that paid off.

"Really? I was just spit-balling. What can you tell me?"

"Well, if the SOB hadn't already been dead, I would have been looking his way for setting the fire we had last September. He was known for it amongst certain types, if you know what I mean. Had a bunch of properties that went up in flames and he used the insurance money to buy more. Although more so than him, he had this nasty little partner. Jack, I think it was."

I swallowed hard and nodded. This was turning weird fast.

"Jack Callen. They had a real estate business together until James filed for Chapter 11. The partner got the business when he died was the way I heard it. "

Shane cocked an eye. "Yeah, well, dig under the surface of that particular scenario and you won't have to look hard for scum. Lots of double dealing, lots of scams, lots of criminal activities, if you know what I mean?"

I did know what he meant but I let him talk. Once he got going, it was tough stopping him. Irishman.

"The other thing I heard was he was involved with those mutts over on Forbes Avenue, that biker gang, the Druids. Illegal drugs and the like. They've got that dive bar that they hang out in over there. Cops are there a couple times a week for one thing or the other, if..."

I said it first. "I know what you mean."

He went on. "Nasty business, Tommy. Low life scum, every one of them. I didn't want to have anything to do with 'em. They came in here and offered to buy me out. Offered a ridiculously low price. Said the neighborhood was getting bad and that this would be my last chance to get out. Getting bad? The neighborhood had just started turning around!"

It was true. The new co-op grocery store they'd built around the corner that was attached to the new luxury condos was doing well. Many were skeptical when they first started going up but the builders filled them pretty quickly. I'd gone into the co-op a couple of times. Not sure who would pay six dollars for a loaf of gluten-free bread but it seemed to be busy every time I went.

I pressed Shane a little. "So, what happened? Did they try to push you around?"

"Yeah, a little...but nothing to write home about. I've seen worse, believe me. Sent some of those biker goons over here to try and start some shit but I get a lot of New Haven's finest in here, both off duty and on...so no one was gonna mess with us. Of course, until that idiot upstairs fell asleep with a cigarette going and burned the place up! If it wasn't for bad luck..."

I nodded but my head was elsewhere. The Druids had a bad reputation. Supposedly the source for most of the meth in the city. I thought back to the "funny" aromas Miriam noticed coming from David's room.

Shane had topped me off again. My third. "Up the Queen!" I toasted, threw down a twenty and left, heading down to Diesel. I was going to start earning that cash. Eventually.

SIX

I started running over things in my head on the walk over to Diesel. It felt confusing, like a lot of little pieces to a big puzzle that had come at me quickly in a very short time. A routine missing person job that was turning into something bigger. The three shots of Jameson weren't helping with my clarity, either.

Diesel Lounge was down in the part of State Street that had been in the process of gentrification for the last 20 years. It never seemed to take. There were a number of so-so restaurants, a florist, a French Patisserie, a coffee roaster, some Chinese take-out joints, some Mexican take-out joints, and Diesel. Somewhere down the line, it had gone from being a bar to a "lounge". Diesel Lounge. Most felt it just enabled them to charge a few more bucks for fancy watered down drinks.

I walked in and it took me a few seconds for my eyes to adjust to the lighting. Bright lights set against copper and steel and chrome. A tin roof. Ultra-hip. Too hip for me. I wasn't sure if I was in a bar or on the set of the next "Fifty Shades" movie.

It was early, before 8, and there weren't a lot of people there. Three girls, probably Yale students, were at one of the two high-tops in the back. There were two young guys at the bar, one at the last seat, one at the first seat. Bookends. I sat down right in the middle.

There was a huge mirror over most of the bar, hung on a slant. You couldn't really see yourself in it so I wondered what it was for. Maybe to make the bar look bigger.

The bartender came over. She was maybe twenty-two and had the kind of hair that takes hours to get just right, so she could look like she just rolled out of the sack.

"Drink?"

"I certainly do...but not just yet. Can I get a ginger ale?"

I could swear I heard a snicker but I looked at both bookends and they were deep into their smartphones, texting or sexting or whatever it is these millennials do. I would lay good money they rarely made calls with them.

"Here you go. I'm Amy, if you want something real later on," and turned to walk away.

"Whoa, hold up a sec. Can I ask you a few questions?" It came out a little too aggressive and I made a mental note to tone it down a bit, at least until the Jameson started to wear off.

"Is that Amy with a Y or do you do the "ie" thing?" Jeez, if there was a bell that measured lameness, I would be ringing it like an altar boy.

"It's a Y. Amy with a Y."

She was smiling but it was a tolerant smile, like she really didn't need this tonight.

"Amy with a Y. Got it. Do you know Marissa Grant? She still works here?"

The smile disappeared immediately and a cold look replaced it.

"She doesn't work here anymore. Do you want to talk to the manager?"

The abrupt change took me aback for a second. There was a story here.

"Well, I'd rather talk to you. Is that okay?"

She walked away, tossing over her shoulder, "I'll get the manager," and disappeared through a door near the back. Thirty seconds later, a guy walked out of the same door and came over to the bar.

"Something I can help you with? You are...?" He was trying to project a no-nonsense attitude but was coming off as rude. I decided to dazzle him with metaphysics.

"I am. And you are?"

He looked confused but composed himself quickly.

"I'm Dino. This is my place. What do you need, Mr....?"

"Shore. I'm trying to locate the son of a client. His name is David Ross. He used to go out with a woman who worked here, according to your website. Marissa Grant. Is she still here?"

He ignored that question. "So, you're with the police?"

I was getting annoyed with the back and forth. "Nope, private. Does she still work here?"

"No, I let Marissa go a few weeks ago. There were a number of 'incidents', money missing from the till, some unsavory types hanging around and talking to her. There may have been some illegal things going on as well. I didn't want that sort of business in here so I let her go. Haven't seen her or her boyfriend since."

Making the rabbit ears sign with his fingers when he said "incidents" made me dislike him even more. I knew there wasn't a lot I was going to get out of him.

"Did she leave a forwarding address maybe, for her last check?"

"No, she picked that up the next day. Came here riding on the back of a loud Harley with one of those biker guys from that gang in East Haven or wherever. Made a lot of noise, both when they pulled up outside and when she came in here. Rude."

Amy, the bartender with a Y, had come back out of the backroom and had sidled up to the end of the bar, within earshot. I looked over at her but she gave no sign she would be giving me the clues that would unlock the whole thing so I could just spend the money and go home and sleep.

I looked at Dino. "Is Dino really your name?"

He blushed a little. "It is. My mother was a big fan of Dean Martin."

"Huh. Count your blessings she didn't like Hoagy Carmichael. Thanks for your help."

I blew Amy with a Y a kiss. "Later, Doll, great talking to ya!" A little sarcasm always goes a long way.

She grimaced and went back to the Yale girls to see if they needed anything.

I tossed down my ginger ale like I was John Wayne, turned and walked out.

SEVEN

I paused on the sidewalk outside of Diesel, trying to figure out my next move. There was a walkway on the side of the building that lead to a small patio in back where they kept their dumpster and where the staff took their cigarette breaks. I heard a noise and looked to see Amy beckoning me over. She met me half way down the walk.

"Call me later, this is my home phone," she said in a whisper, handing me a slip of paper. Then went back into the bar. I smiled. Still got it.

I decided to walk up Elm Street and check out Donut Crazy, the last place David worked. My first thought was that it wouldn't be much help. My second thought was I was hungry.

Taking Elm Street took me through one of my favorite parts of the city. New Haven is basically laid out in a four-by-four grid, with the Green at the center. One of the first planned cities in America, it had been founded in 1638 by the Puritans. Some of them still lived here.

New Haven is also home to Yale University, although some say that, these days, Yale is home to New Haven. The school started buying up property early on and has yet to stop. They have their own security force, they own every major building in the city, and they provide housing for more than 16,000 students. They also employ 4500 people as part of the faculty. If someone was selling something people wanted, there were a lot of potential customers.

The walk took me past the Court House, where, in the sixties, Bobby Seale had been tried for being black. It was a grand old building, but was constantly surrounded by scaffolding as they tried to repair a building that had once been targeted for demolition. New Haven has always been slow to give up the ghost on all things old.

After that came the Graduate Club. There were a number of these "social" clubs in New Haven that belonged to Yale and this was one of the more elite ones. I was hoping there'd be some graduates hanging outside that I could banter with but it was too cold. In the summer, they would sit on the steps, discussing Dickensian literature or the humor found in the writings of John Maynard Keynes. Always good for a chat.

I walked up Elm to York and turned right. Crossing the street, I noticed a crowd of kids queuing up for a show at Toad's Place. Started originally as a blues club where Willie Dixon and Muddy Waters played, it soon became home to a million great shows in the 70s and the 80's. Lots of top acts who would play the New Haven Coliseum liked to show up after the show and do another set. The Stones did it. Springsteen did it. Dylan and U2 did it. The place had a capacity of under a thousand but filled it way past that number for those shows. Some issues with serving underage kids and the place was closed down for a while. It reopened but was never the same again. Now all they featured were cover bands and rap DJs.

Donut Crazy was a recent addition to the block. It was a small chain that started in CT and now had five locations in the state. With donuts that tasted like PBJs or resembled red velvet cake. Buying a dozen required a second mortgage but I had to admit, they were mighty tasty. And it felt right at home next to the Greek pizza joint and Blue State, another upscale coffee house.

I went in. The crowd was typical to every coffee shop in New Haven. Four overstuffed couches, each holding four students, all looking intently at four laptops. They were oblivious to anything going on around them, much more interested in finding out who did what to whom and when. I often thought they were probably emailing the person that was sitting right next to them.

I went to the counter and waited my turn. When the two girls in front of me finally made their choice (Butternut, upset at the lack of any gluten-free donuts), the kid working the counter looked right at me and yelled, "Next!" loudly. I turned my head both ways, feigning surprise that it was my turn. "Me?"

"What can I get cha, dude?" I paused. He was Jeff Spicoli, come to life. He had a great shock of dyed blond hair, corn-rowed and then piled up on his head like a turban. He had on a tie-dyed Grateful Dead shirt and that cloudy look in his eyes that told me he'd spent his break "relaxing" in the alley in the back. He also looked like he weighed three hundred and thirty pounds, so it was solid bet that he ate his paycheck in donuts every day. Most likely after the alley visit.

"Whattya need, Bro?"

I smiled. "I need to speak to the manager, Bro."

He pulled back a little. "Oh...okay, cool. I'll get her."

He went into a small office near the back and then came out quickly, followed by a large black woman.

"Hello, I'm Sandra Baker, the night manager. Can I help you?" Very business-like and to the point. There must be a school these managers go to.

"Yes, Tommy Shore. I'm looking for some information about an ex-employee, David Ross. Worked here but not that far back. Anything you can give me would be a great help. He's missing and his mother hired me to find him before she called the cops." Might as well get it all in rather than wait for the inevitable questions.

"Oh, David doesn't work here anymore."

David. She said it slowly, her voice dripping with disappointment. I sighed.

"Yes, I know, that's the whole "ex-employee" thing. I was hoping you might have some information on him, a forwarding address or a contact number?"

She pretended to think and actually looked up at the ceiling. I felt lucky she didn't stroke her chin.

"I don't think so but come back into my office and I'll look."

She opened a hinged half-door to let me back.

"Watch your step. There's sugar all over the floor. Can't have any accidents."

I almost said that washing them might be a good way to prevent that from happening but I stopped myself. I needed to see what she might tell me.

The office was tiny and the two of us being back there filled it up uncomfortably. There was a stench of cooking oil and cheap perfume, mixed with leather that's been sat upon too long without cleaning. I started to get claustrophobic and nauseous at the same time.

She pulled a ledger down from a small shelf over the desk and leafed through it, pretending to search. When she got to the tab with the letter R, she smiled and actually said, "A-ha, here it is," then gave me the same number that Miriam had given me for her phone. I pretended to write it down. I was getting tired of dead ends.

"Okay, thanks," I said, giving her my card and asking her to call me if she found anything else. I think she nodded but I was up and out the door and didn't look back. But I stopped at the counter and bought a maple-glazed bacon donut. Research.

Outside, I checked my phone. Reilly had texted and wanted me to meet him at the Owl. Always a good idea. A cigar and a shot, then bed. It was starting to feel like a long day.

EIGHT

Reilly was sitting in his usual seat, the one my ex always used to take, at the far end of the bar and the only one facing the door. If it was occupied when he came in, he would sit as close to it as possible and stare intently until the person (or persons) got uncomfortable and left. I'd seen him do it a dozen times. No one ever wants to mess with crazy.

There was a seat open right next to him. No one usually wants to sit near crazy, either. Except other crazies. And me.

"What's shakin', Hoss?"

He looked up from his gluten-free Omission beer. It took a minute for his eyes to focus. A glimmer of recognition finally settled in. He'd been here a while.

"Tommy! Oi, fuckin' Oi! You're here! Shots?"

It was probably the last thing he needed but I said sure. He beckoned for Joe, the Friday night bartender. "Joe, shots!"

Joe was a good-looking kid who loved movies, basketball and his fiancé, possibly in that order. He was constantly pounding a bottle of Kombucha he bought by the case at a health food store near here. He was easy going until he wasn't.

Joe put two shot glasses in front of us and poured from the bottle of Jameson that was already nearby. "This is it, Seamus, last one."

I looked up and smiled. Nobody ever really used Reilly's first name. Joe made it work.

"No more, understood?" Both Seamus and Joe were smiling but you could cut the underlying tension with a butter knife.

Reilly relaxed first and said, "Not a problem, Joseph." You could tell he wanted more but he got tired early these days. It was just shy of 11:00. We downed the shots.

The Owl was jumping. Being the only bar in CT that allowed both smoking AND drinking had its perks, and people came from all over the state. The air was thick with a heady mix of cigar smoke, cigarette smoke, sweat and expectations. It wasn't a pickup bar but I'd watched many a one-night hookup that happens here on Friday nights.

I turned to Reilly. "Okay, Hoss, concentrate...did you find out anything? About the case?"

He tried to focus. It wasn't easy. He was fighting something that none of the brilliant Yale doctors had yet to identify. He'd been poked and prodded for years. Whatever it was had taken a toll on his body and on his mind. Concentration wasn't a strong suit.

"I did, I did. Give me a second." Joe had set me up with a club soda back, slice of lemon, no straw. I sipped a little and waited.

Seamus had been bent forward in his seat, his head

an inch from his empty shot glass. Thinking. He shot up quickly.

"Yes! Yes, I did. City Hall. I went there."

I waited. It took time with Reilly but it was usually worth it.

"Spoke to your buddy, Sean. He said thanks for the tix. Ross. Ross. I was looking for a background on a guy named Ross. James?"

I nodded and waited. I could see the light go on in his eyes.

"Oi, that guy's a real piece of work. Sean told me there were lots of shady deals. A few fires and insurance claims. Bunches of different corporation names. Had a partner. Colon or something?"

"Callen."

"Yeah, that it's. Sounded like an asshole." He laughed at his joke. I was appreciative but any acknowledgement would throw him off. He continued.

"He's a real piece of work. Had some trouble in Rhode Island but never did any time. Embezzlement or the like, in the 80s. Ross was the front man because of the other git's background."

I thought about all this for a second. The Rhode Island stuff was intriguing. It told me that the guy wasn't above doing whatever necessary to make money. Wondered if David knew about his dad.

Reilly bolted up suddenly, grabbed his floor-length leather from the back of chair, slipped it on in one quick move, and said, "I'm outta here. Sleeping in tomorrow so don't call until after 2. You around?"

I shrugged. Not sure where the day would take me. Besides, I had a date. Which I'd only just remembered.

"Got a date tomorrow night. I'm going do some

more digging during the day. You'll be here tomorrow night?"

"Yep. My sister's in town. We're gonna get dinner and hang here. Later."

And left. Who was that masked man?

I sipped my club soda and pondered another shot. That would make five. One toke over the line. I got the check (which included Reilly's drinks), paid Joe with some of the change from the hundred, and left. I walked across the street to my apartment. Ah, the joys of city living.

I considered trying to read. I was in the middle of a classic, James Crumley's "The Last Good Kiss". I'd read it before but he was one of my favorites and I tried to read his books over again ever few years. He and I had had a drink together many years ago, when I was on drive-about in Montana. It was one of the highlights of my life.

I was much too tired. The four shots had taken hold and I had a long day tomorrow. When I was younger, I could get by on six hours of sleep. These days, I could barely stay awake for six hours.

I undressed, threw on some sweats and a t-shirt and got into bed. I was asleep before my head hit the pillow.

NINE

I awoke with a start. I had been dreaming that I was being chased by pygmies. Dressed in black Hugo Boss suits. Indiana Jones meets a Robert Palmer video. They had been throwing donuts at me. When I came to a cliff, I had to make a choice. I'd reached in my jacket pocket but my whip was gone. The only thing there was a piece of paper with a name and number on it. I woke up and realized I had forgotten to call Amy, the bartender at Diesel.

I looked at the clock by the bed. 7:30. Not too bad. I laid there another few minutes, stretching, then got out of bed.

My head was a little fuzzy. I usually drank a lot of water before I went to sleep if I'd been drinking but I was too tired last night. Now there was this dull ache between my eyes. Note to self: Go easy on the Jameson until the case ends.

I went to my small galley kitchen and ground some beans to make a pot of good coffee in the small French press. A third of Peet's Major Dickinson, a third of Starbuck's Christmas blend, and a third Dunkin' Donuts. Yes, D&D. I couldn't drink the coffee they sold in the stores anymore but the beans they sold in the supermarket smoothed the other roasts out. Coffee was one of my many weaknesses.

I'd started drinking coffee mixed into my milk as a kid. My uncle Ray would babysit for us and he got me hooked on it. Soon there was less milk and lots more coffee.

On the road as a publisher's rep in the 80s, it was a survival tactic to find the best cup around. My territory had been New England and upstate NY. This was long before the "coffee boom" happened and most of the swill available was either too weak or the 500- mile stuff they sold at truck stops. When the boom hit, it was as if the coffee gods had answered my prayers. Soon there would be a Starbucks on every corner. Hell, New Haven had two of them, two blocks apart from each other, along with the 10 other places.

After the water boiled and I poured it over the mix, the aroma helped to soothe my headache. I let it steep for three minutes then poured the first cup of the day. Black. That first sip was always nirvana. I sat down and contemplated what had transpired so far.

There was still that nagging underbelly to this thing that wasn't sitting right. Every piece of information we uncovered seemed to open up another dark corner.

I found the piece of paper with Amy's number on it but it was too early to call. She'd probably worked until closing time, 2:00 am for most of the bars here. It would have to wait a few hours.

I had more questions for Miriam. I found my pad

and dialed the number she'd given me. A woman answered on the second ring.

"Ross/Callen residence."

It threw me. I had thought that the number she had given me was her cell phone, but this sounded like a land line. And it didn't sound like her.

"Uh, Miriam Ross, please?"

"This is she."

Huh. Different persona at home. I wondered if she was always this formal.

"Tommy Shore."

"Oh, hello Mr. Shore. I'm so sorry, I didn't recognize the number."

"No worries, I'm happy to do it the old way and introduce myself. Listen, I have some questions and some information. Do you have time to meet this afternoon?"

She paused. I could sense her weighing the question.

"Well, I'm having a party for some people here at my home today and really need to be here for the caterers. Do you think you can you come to my home?"

A party? Clearly heartbroken. Given what was going on, a party was a little strange.

I would need to borrow a car from my friend Kevin. He usually stayed home on Saturdays now that he had the kid. College football from noon to dark. I could borrow his car. There'd be a price to pay but he was usually good about it.

"Sure, I can come there." She gave me the address. It was out in Hamden. She started to give me directions but I cut her off. "I've got GPS, I'll find it. See you at noon?" She agreed, said goodbye and hung up. Very proper, very civil, very distant.

I called Kevin as soon as I hung up. "What!??" Kevin had two speaking voices, loud and bellow.

"Hey, it's me, T. Can I use your car for a few hours?"

I heard a muffled noise, like he'd put the phone against his shirt. Sounded vaguely like "mummer-futkrr." Then he came back on. "Why?"

This was the dance we did every time I asked for his car. My beat-up 2004 Camry has given up the ghost a few months back and I decided then that I didn't need to pay the taxes, pay for parking, pay for maintenance, and have a car payment if I was living in the city. The walking would be good for me. The only difficulty was when I needed to drive someplace far. I had been using Uber a lot but that had gotten expensive for distances. And I wanted to be able to make a quick getaway.

"I've got a gig and need to go to Hamden. Should only be a few hours."

Kevin also had two moods. Aggravated and more aggravated. I could tell he was somewhere in between.

"Okay, okay. How ya gonna get here?" Kevin lived in an old two-story house in the Wooster Square area.

"I'll walk down. I need to get breakfast and it'll be good to clear my head with a walk. Does two hours or so work for you, say 10:30, 11?"

He agreed but demanded I bring him a bacon, egg and cheese sandwich. He'd known me a long time and knew that I would be stopping somewhere, a creature of habit.

I liked this new place on Crown Street called Meat and Co. They were an offshoot of 168 Crown, a restaurant next door with a bar out of Star Wars and really strange booths. The food at the restaurant was too weird for me but the deli they'd opened made great sandwiches.

I showered quickly, got dressed and left the apartment building. It had warmed up a bit and the sun was doing its best to try to come out.

Might just end up a good Saturday.

TEN

I went down the alleyway by my apartment and came out on Temple Street. At the end of the alley on the right was the Temple Grill and on the left was a new Middle Eastern joint that I had yet to try. Temple Street had blown up with restaurants in the last decade, none of them all that great. Besides those two, there was a burger joint, an Ethiopian place, a Thai takeout place, a Greek restaurant and a Spanish restaurant. The city was doing its best to be international and cosmopolitan but, as usual, fell a little short.

I hit Crown Street at a full gait. The deli was down a way, across Church Street. Waiting to cross, I glanced to my right and looked over at the Ethiopian Embassy. I snorted out loud. Here, in New Haven, an Ethiopian embassy. For all seven of the Ethiopians that lived in the city. It never failed to amuse me.

I walked into Meat and Co. to a warm greeting from John, one of the owners.

"Tommy Boy! What's up, my man?"

He was a big guy, maybe 250, 6'2, and gregarious.

He treated all of his customers like he had been waiting all morning just to see them.

"Hey John. SOSDD, my friend, like always. And you?"

"Living the dream, T, living the dream. Usual?"

I held up two fingers. "I need an extra one today, John. Car rental fee."

He laughed like he understood what I meant and started making our breakfast. I looked around at all the different offerings and made a mental note to stop here for a sandwich one day soon.

Breakfast was ready in ten minutes so I paid him and then continued my walk down towards Wooster Street.

Wooster Street was an area of New Haven that had always been famous for two things, pizza and cherry blossoms. Each year, they held the Cherry Blossom festival there. A hundred thousand people crammed into a few small blocks. It was typically chaos.

The residents also held the Avest there, the Italian Festival. At one time, the Italian section of town was the safest area in the city. Protected. Two of New Haven's most storied pizza parlors were there, Sally's and Pepe's. At Sally's, you needed to know someone to get in and get any kind of service. At Pepe's, you almost always waited in a line. Pepe's had a sister place behind it called The Spot, who made their living off of the overflow from Pepe's and the mooks who couldn't bear to wait in the line.

You were either in the Pepe's camp or in the Sally's camp. Personally, I liked Modern on State Street more than either one. You didn't have to deal with the elitist bullshit at Sally's or with the corporate changes that

Pepe's went through when the original owner sold out to a restaurant group. There was a Pepe's at the Indian casino now, for chrissakes.

I cut through the park. The cherry blossoms were just starting to open and would be in full bloom by early May. It was a great place for a walk.

When I got a half block away from Kevin's, I could already hear the Grateful Dead playing. Loud. Kevin loved the Dead, Wilco and a few more bands but had no patience for any other music. He listened with the stereo turned up to 11. By the time I reached his house, it sounded even louder.

I knocked, hard. Nothing. Knocked again. Harder. I heard the music being turned down to 10 and the door flung open.

"What!! What!!? Oh, hey Tom, it's you. C'mon in."

Kevin was another pal from the Owl. He used to come in to the bar a lot but then he and the woman he lived with had a son a few years back and he had since changed his drinking habits accordingly. He still drank as much, he just did it at home. He drove a truck for a local liquor distributor and got a hefty "discount" on all the small batch stuff that was the rage these days. I considered him a good friend.

"Want a beer? I got all kinds, IPAs, Brown ales, might even have a porter or two. Anything?"

It was barely 10:30 in the morning so I passed. I took the sandwiches out of the bag I was carrying and asked if he had coffee. He looked at me like I had grown a second head.

"What do you think?" he sneered.

Didn't matter. I'd stop for one on the road. "Can I grab your keys?"

He reached in his pants pocket and tossed a huge key ring at me.

"Bring it back with the tank full, yeah? It's the key with the tape on it."

I caught the ring in midair and looked for the taped key. I wrapped my sandwich back up, said "Thanks" and went out the front door. I heard the volume go back up before I reached the car door.

The car was a Subaru Impreza, maybe 5 years old. I got in and it started right up. I drove around the block and back to State Street, then cut over to Orange Street and Nico's Market. I went in, grabbed a large, freshly-roasted Colombian coffee and then got back on State until I picked up Interstate 91. I ate the sandwich and drank the coffee as I drove.

I'd put her address into the GPS on my phone and the cheeky phone voice woman took me onto the Hamden connector, down Route 10, and up into the backwoods until I reached an area of newly built McMansions. Thankfully, the leaves weren't completely out on the trees or I would have never found the place.

The house was enormous, maybe 10 rooms and a lot of land. Way too much house for just a mother and son. Maybe they took in boarders?

I parked at the end of the driveway and got out. Looking around, I could see the catering trucks in the back, unloading. There was also a new BMW 750 parked in front of me in the driveway and a small Audi r3 next to it. Expensive rides.

I walked up the front sidewalk and rang the door-bell. I heard loud footsteps on hardwood floors. The door opened and the man standing in front of me said, "Deliveries are in back."

I knew who it was immediately. Might have been his demeanor, maybe his cock of the walk attitude, or maybe the copious amount of hair gel.

"No, I'm Tom Shore, I'm here to see Miriam. Can you get her for me?"

"Oh, right. The guy that Miriam hired to find David." He stuck out his hand. "Glad to meet you. Jack Callen."

Saturday was going south quickly.

ELEVEN

He was a lot shorter than I thought he'd be, maybe 5′7 in shoes. He also looked oilier than I had originally imagined. When he'd thrust out his hand to introduce himself, I had been wary about shaking it. I hated the feel of oil on my skin. But I shook it anyway.

"How's it going? Is Miriam here?" All business.

He was smiling but not in a friendly way and looked at me a beat longer than I liked.

"Yeah, I'll get her."

I stayed outside. I hadn't been invited in but then I hadn't planned on going in anyway.

Miriam came to the door a minute later.

"Hello, Mr. Shore. You're early. I believe you said noon?"

"Yeah, well, the early bird catches the worm and all that. Speaking of which, isn't that your dead husband's ex-partner?"

She squirmed a little. Talking to the help.

"It is. Jack and I were friends before James passed and after he died, Jack helped me out quite a bit. I'm not sure how this is any of your business though, Mr. Shore."

So much for winning hearts and minds.

"It's not, really, but I always like to consider all the information I get, even if it's thrown in my face. Can we talk out here?"

I motioned towards the car. My first sense from meeting Callen was that he'd have no trouble hiding behind the door to listen in to the conversation.

She turned and looked back into the house, considered her options, then closed the door behind her and stepped out onto the front stoop.

I walked over to the Subaru and leaned on the right fender, folded my arms and waited. She paused then followed me. Doesn't miss a trick, this one.

She was wearing a pair of black Capris and a light blue blouse that looked like it was silk. Tied together with sensible Louis Vuitton loafers. All very expensive. Must be her "home for the caterers" outfit.

I decided to tell her what I knew before I asked her any of my questions. It would put her mind at ease that I was actually earning my money.

I told her about Diesel and about Donut Crazy, where I'd come up with nothing. I told her that there were some other leads I would be following but that there was nothing to report as of yet. She nodded the entire time as she listened but I could tell her mind was somewhere else. She glanced back at the house a few times. I followed her glance and thought I saw the curtains in what must have been the front room move a little.

"I need to ask you a few questions, Mrs. Ross. Okay?"

Trying to get her focused on me.

She nodded but quickly added, "It needs to be quick. I have 80 people due here tonight for cocktails and a buffet dinner. It's being catered by the Union League in New Haven. Do you know it?"

I ignored the underlying condescension and nodded. I ate there once a month and was taking my date there tonight.

"I do know it. It's one of my favorite places in the city for dinner. I didn't realize they catered."

She seemed surprised that I knew the place but continued on.

"They usually don't but this is a very special occasion. Jack is announcing his candidacy for mayor of New Haven and there will be a large number of very influential people here tonight. All of them donors."

Now it was my turn to be surprised. A number of thoughts quickly crossed my mind. I had assumed that, given what Reilly told me, Callen's background would be a major obstacle towards getting a driver's license, let alone running for office. I'd also assumed that there had been money issues. No campaign I'd ever read about was run without lots and lots of dollars.

I looked at her closely. In the light of the day, I could see she was older than I first thought, early fifties. Must have had David later in life.

I asked my questions.

"You told me that you and David had words before he left. What did he say or do when you confronted him about the stuff you found in his room?"

She looked at me. Her demeanor said it was painful for her but that she was doing her best to keep a "Stiff upper lip."

"He denied that there was anything wrong. Said they weren't his drugs, that he only smoked a little pot."

I nodded. I realized immediately this was going to be a dead end. She had a part she needed to play. I continued on anyway.

"His girlfriend actually worked at Diesel until recently. Did he ever mention why she left there?"

She scowled. "I was not a fan of hers, Mr. Shore. She was..." She was searching for the right word.

"...common. We never really discussed her. He mentioned Diesel a few times, usually on his way out the door, when he was evidently headed there."

I nodded again.

"This one might be difficult. Can I ask you when and how James died?" I'd read the obit but I wanted to hear it from her.

She blanched a bit. Her eyes got moist. I was jaded so I thought she was putting it on for me. I also thought she could give Meryl Streep a run for the Oscar.

"He died two years ago, this coming week. In a fire at one of his properties. It was the most horrible time of my life."

I tried to keep a blank face. Given the stuff I'd heard at Trinity, the fact that his death was fire related didn't surprise me.

I took it all in, said thank you and told her that I would be in touch. She looked back at the house, turned back to me, and whispered, "Mr. Shore, please be careful? I only want you to find David and let me know where he is. Nothing more. Do not confront him. Once you do find him, please just let me know that he's safe and I'll take it from there. I don't want any more attention paid to this business than there has to be. It can cause some major problems for me."

I nodded a third time. I was getting good at it. Maybe there was some money to be made in competitive nodding.

I got into Kevin's car, pulled out of the driveway, and headed back down the road, towards civilization.

I never noticed the black sedan following me.

TWELVE

I called Reilly first even though it was only 12:30 and
he had warned me to wait until 2.

"Yo, Tommy here. You up?"

I heard voices in the background. His voice was
raspy.

"Yeah, I'm up, I'm up. Where are you?"

"Driving back from Hamden. Lots to tell. Can you
meet me? I'll buy you a Louie's."

Always good to go with the food bribe right from
the jump.

"Sure. When? I've got some company here but she's
leaving in a few."

We decided to meet at 1:30 at Louie's Lunch. I was
already hungry.

I hung up and pulled in to the Starbucks on
Dixwell Avenue in Hamden. I wasn't usually a fan of
their regular coffee but I liked their Americanos.

Parking was always hard to find there so I pulled
into one of the spots that had signs that read "Dry
Cleaners Only - All Others Will Be Towed at Driver's

Expense." I wouldn't be long so I ignored the sign and went in.

It was a typical Starbucks scenario. Every chair and table was occupied, each person staring at a laptop or smartphone screen, an oversized coffee drink close by. It was library quiet, save for the insipid music playing overhead and the occasional whirr of the coffee grinder/espresso machines. I walked to the counter. A pretty young girl with pink striped hair smiled at me.

"What can we make for you today?"

Her name was Nicole. Her apron told me so.

"Well, I would like a large Americano quad, four shots, a little bit of heavy cream and some room, please?"

"Grande or Venti... and your name, Sir?"

I loved doing this dance, it was a source of constant amusement to me.

"Large."

Nicole grimaced. I could tell she just wanted to go somewhere and stare at her smartphone. I relented.

"Grande. Name's Tommy."

I waited and gazed around while the "barista", Greg, made my coffee. I laughed to myself and thought it was a good thing that they didn't require to see a laptop before they would serve me.

Greg yelled out my name, I grabbed the cup, and walked out to the car.

I had to put the cup on the roof of the car to get out the keys when I first noticed the black sedan. It had dark tinted windows and had been circling the building. It was meant to look like a driver trying to find a space but when I pointed at the car to signal that I was leaving, it picked up speed and rolled past me. I turned to watch it and saw Rhode Island plates. It struck me as strange. It was a straight shot down I95 from Rhode Island, which went by the harbor on the other side of New Haven. With plenty of Starbucks on that side of town. You didn't have to come anywhere near Hamden. I guess they could have been visiting somebody but something felt off about it.

I sat in Kevin's car and sipped my coffee. It was scalding hot so I took the lid off and let it cool. Then took out the piece of paper and dialed Amy from Diesel Lounge. A child answered.

"Hello?"

"Oh, hi there. Is Amy home, is your mom home?" She hadn't looked old enough to have a kid that was old enough to answer the phone but who knew these days.

I could hear giggling. "Well, which one do you want? My mom's not home but my sister Amy is."

"Your sister would be great. Can I talk to her?"

I heard the phone bang against a wall and heard a muffled yell, "AMY!!"

Thirty seconds later I heard a woman's voice. "This is Amy."

"Amy with a Y. Tommy Shore. We met last night at your bar. I was asking about Marissa Grant. You gave me this number and told me to call you?"

A pause. "Yes, I remember. I thought that you would call me last night. I overheard you and Dino talking. He gave you part of the story but there's more to it than he gave you. I liked Marissa. She was a friend and I think you need to hear the whole story. She deserves that."

I apologized for not calling her last night. Clearly

not getting points for waiting until a reasonable hour to call her today.

"What is it you want to tell me?"

She lowered her voice. "Not on the phone. Can you meet me before my shift? I go in around 6:30."

I had a date for 7 but I needed to hear what she had to say.

"How about we meet tomorrow instead, at Willoughby's on Grove around 5:00, before your shift? Do you work on Sunday?"

Willoughby was yet another artisanal coffee shop. I'd always thought someone should open one and call it "Grounds for Divorce."

She said yes, she was working and agreed to meet me at the coffee shop. I wrote it down on my pad and we hung up. I backed out of the space slowly, careful not to hit the minions heading into Starbucks, pulled out onto Dixwell Avenue and headed back to New Haven.

About 4 miles down the avenue, Hamden turned into New Haven. You had to go through an area called Highwood and the changes that had occurred there were always striking to me. In its heyday, it had been a great neighborhood with a drugstore, a small grocery store, and a number of nice two-family homes for its blue-collar residents. It had taken a beating in the 80s when there was easy money everywhere and people had become upwardly mobile. It was mostly low-income housing now and every other storefront was a bodega, a check cashing joint, a liquor store or a church, with names like "Upon this Rock" or "The World of God".

I veered left when the road split and stayed on that

street until I hit Elm Street and the parking lot for the strip of stores there. Keeping to the right, I merged onto the other side of Elm and drove down to College, then right onto Crown. I pulled into the parking lot next to where Louie's was, took a ticket from the machine, and then parked as close to the building as the attendant would let me. It was all automated except for the guys who pointed you to spaces.

As I walked over the gravel lot, I looked across the street at BAR.

BAR was a club/pizza joint/brewery that had live music on the weekends and was a favorite of both the Yale students and the people coming into the city from the surrounding towns. That combination rarely worked well once alcohol was applied and the cops were always being called there. I knew one of the guys who occasionally worked the door and I was looking to see if he was on when I saw the black sedan go by.

With Rhode Island plates.

THIRTEEN

I watched as it went past me and then turned right at High Street. Maybe it was a coincidence and I was just being paranoid, but in the words of Kurt Cobain, just because you're paranoid don't mean they're not after you.

I caught the last two letters on the plate but couldn't see it all. LX. I took out my pad, wrote it down, and went into Louie's.

Louie's Lunch was one of my favorite places to meet. It had been around New Haven forever and was recognized by the Library of Congress as the birthplace of the hamburger. Started by a blacksmith in 1895, it had been in 3 different locations around the city. They actually picked up the entire building to move it each time and it had been in this spot since 1975. It was a rite of passage for every citizen of New Haven to experience Louie's at least once. I was there a few times a month.

Reilly had scored one of the two small face to face booths in the place, on the left, near the counter. I wasn't a fan of the community table on the other side of the tiny restaurant or of the little single booths that they must have purchased from the Spanish Inquisition, so I was happy.

I sat down just as they called out Reilly's name. He was looking at his phone and didn't look up, but told me, "Pay the man." I got back up and paid the kid at the counter, who handed me four paper plates, each holding a juicy burger, with the works. White toast, meat, onions, a tomato slice and cheese spread. No condiments of any kind. Regular patrons know that one was never enough. I also grabbed two root beers. Reilly finally looked up in disdain at the soda.

He ate most of his first one in record time. I watched in awe.

"Jeez, hungry much?"

He swallowed the last bite. "I am. Had quite the workout last night."

I really didn't want the details of his evening but I knew that trying to stop him from telling me about it was an act of futility.

"Used to be a gymnastics coach at UConn. My god, I never realized the human body could bend like that!"

I did what I do best. I nodded.

Then he asked me, "So, what's going on with our case?"

I was surprised the gymnast story ended so quickly. He must be tired. I was also surprised that it was now "our" case.

I told him what happened over the last 24 hours and he listened intently. I could tell he was intrigued.

"Man, that's awesome. This is a real case!"

I needed to curb his enthusiasm a bit. It was still too early.

"Maybe. It's early. Monday, I need you to go over to the Register and find my buddy Billy C. He'll give you access to the archives. I want everything you can find on the Callen guy. Something's definitely not Kosher with this guy."

Reilly agreed. He'd already finished his other burger. I still had a half left from my second. He pointed at it and asked if I was going to eat it. I motioned for him to take it. "Be my guest." It was gone in seconds. Gymnasts.

I continued. "There's one other thing. I didn't see it until I stopped in Hamden at Starbucks for coffee, but I think I'm being followed. Black sedan, Buick maybe, Rhode Island plates. Think it cruised by me as I was coming in here."

He was dismayed and intrigued simultaneously, shaking his head in disbelief.

"Why do you insist on going to those places for that corporate swill? There's hippies there!"

He paused a second from his usual Starbucks diatribe. "The car... you get a number?"

I shook my head. "Nah, it went by too fast, before I realized it was the same car. I did get the last two letters."

He had his head in his hand, upset at my lack of sleuthing skills. I tried to pacify him. I was getting tired but still had some errands to run.

"I know, I know. But just be careful, yeah?"

He looked at me for a good two minutes before he spoke.

"Oi, let's get a drink."

The last thing I needed. "I can't. Got a date tonight. Going to Union League with Rosalind, that nurse I met a few weeks back."

He was smiling now.

"Oh yeah, the one who came to the Owl. Really pretty, a little older? I liked her. She was a good sport."

He had been on a rant that night. Communism, hippies, socialism, the Sex Pistols, doctors, lawyers, ex-wives, kids...no topic was safe. Fueled by Mr. Jameson, of course.

She was there with friends and was sitting at the bar. I was sitting next to her and we chatted. She had asked me if he was always like that and I had replied that he was. That opened the door and we talked for an hour before one of her friends said she needed to leave. I asked her for her number and if she would like to have dinner with me sometime and she said she would, to call her.

Tonight would be that sometime.

Reilly unfolded his lanky frame from the small booth and stood up. His head almost hit the ceiling.

"I'm off like a prom dress. Maybe later for a drink? Bring her along, she has smiley eyes."

I told him I would try but that I actually hoped I would be busy most of the night. He laughed, clapped me on the back and left.

I left a minute later, got the car from the lot, and drove down to Kevin's house to drop off the car.

I never saw the black sedan that followed me to Kevin's street.

FOURTEEN

Kevin had texted me that he wasn't going to be home that night and that I was to drop the keys inside the letter slot in the door on the side of the house. It was starting to get dark later now but today it had been overcast by noon and it was already dusky on his street. I parked the car in the space I had picked it up from, went to the side of the house, deposited the keys in the slot, and cut through his backyard to start the walk back to my apartment.

I decided to go by way of Crown Street again so I could stop at The Wine Thief and get something for when (and if) my date came back to my apartment tonight. During our Owl conversation, we had discussed wine and I remembered she said she liked Sauvignon Blanc but hated Chardonnay. She clearly had strong opinions about wine.

I crossed State, walked down to Crown, and turned right at Cafe Nine. The Nine was a tiny showcase club for indie rockers and blues players. Marshall Crenshaw, Richard Lloyd, The Blasters – they'd all played there and tickets were typically just six bucks. They used to serve a killer burger but then re-did the place a few years back and took out the kitchen to get more tables in. They still served popcorn with your drinks, though, and gin and tonics were only $2.50.

I walked up Crown until I got to the Wine Thief. I told the clerk there what I wanted and he showed me a couple of bottles. We settled on a crisp, zesty Fume Blanc from California that went with a lot of different foods. I felt good that she would like it. I thought about getting snacks but after the meal I knew we'd have at Union League, I decided against it.

I let myself in the side door of my building and walked the few stairs up and into my apartment.

I looked around and sighed. I had become a slob. Well, not really, I had just gotten lazy and let things slide a bit. I set about to cleaning up.

Around 5:30, I took a shower and shaved. I had laid out a Midnight blue shirt, black wool slacks, and a black Hugo Boss blazer. The black Allen Edmonds loafers made the outfit complete.

I still had forty-five minutes to kill so I went out the front and next door to the bar at Roia, a French/Italian restaurant that had opened a few years back. I had become friendly with Avi, the Colombian chef/owner and I liked to sit at the bar occasionally for a cocktail. Avi was standing behind the bar, looking at a cookbook when I walked in and looked up and smiled when he saw me, waving me over. I sat down and he greeted me, "Sir. What will be your pleasure tonight?"

"Surprise me." It was a game we played. I knew he liked a challenge. I watched him consider his bar shelves, then grab a bottle of absinthe, some sugar, a small bottle of bitters and a bottle of good Rye.

I smiled at him. "Ah, a Sazerac. Nice."

He smiled back. "Damn... you're good, my friend, you're good."

He was being kind. He knew I had bartended a while back when things were slow.

It was a perfect way to start the night. The sugar mellowed the bitters out and it all blended together to make the perfect drink. It was every bit as good as the ones I'd overindulged in when I was last in New Orleans.

I finished it, threw a twenty on the bar, and got up to leave. He seemed disappointed.

"So soon?"

"Got a date. Going to Union League."

His smile faltered a little but he recovered quickly. Chefs can be competitive.

"Well, have a good time."

"Thanks. Should be great."

I gave him a short salute and left.

Rosalind was waiting for me in front of the Union League. The restaurant was housed in the Sherman Building, which used to be the home of Roger Sherman, a signer of both the Declaration of Independence and the Constitution. Old and charming... like me.

I waved as I got closer. When I reached her, she leaned up and kissed my cheek. Yep, it was going to be a great night.

We went up the steep stairs into the foyer and through the etched glass doors. Jean-Michel greeted us warmly.

"Ah, Monsieur Shore, you're back. It's been awhile,

how have you been?" It sounded so much more sophisti-
cated when said in his thick French accent.

"And who is your beautiful friend?"

"Jean-Michel, this is Rosalind. Rosalind, Jean-
Michel."

"Ah, Rosalind...my mother's name was Rosalind."

Who knew if it was true but I could see she was
charmed.

He took her coat and handed me a ticket. And
winked at me. "Tres beau," he whispered.

He led us to my usual table, just inside the Club
Room, the second table on the left. The bar was behind
me and she sat on the chair next to me so she could see
people as they came through to go to the bar. It was
more casual than the main dining room but still quite
lovely.

I asked her if it would be okay if we let the chef
choose dinner and if there was anything she didn't like
to eat. She shook her head and we told the waiter to ask
Jean-Pierre, a Master French chef, to send whatever he
wanted. She ordered a Kir Royal but I stayed with
water. I still had a buzz from the Sazerac.

"So, tell me about you."

She chuckled softly.

"You get right to it, don't you?"

I smiled. It was the most relaxed I'd felt in a while.

"Why waste time with the small talk when we can
waste time with the big talk?"

She laughed and started telling me about herself;
her nursing career in all parts of the medical field; her
love of good food and her abilities as a great, self-taught
cook; her love of travel and of Paris in particular; her
kids that were spread out around the country; and

briefly about her ex-husband and his untimely death many years back.

I held my own, telling her of my time in the book business; how I came to do PI work; and how we shared the same love of food and travel.

In between these stories of us, the waiter brought us out amazing dishes - cheesy puff pastries as an amuse bouche; a hearty squab soup; Foie Gras and toast points; luscious duck breast in a velvety wine sauce; and profiteroles. The only criticism she had was that they used ice cream instead of French custard in the dessert. But it was still fine.

I asked her if she wanted to have coffee or perhaps an after-dinner glass of wine at my apartment and she agreed. I paid the check and was getting her coat when my cell phone rang. I hesitated a moment but knew I had to answer it. It was Reilly.

"Get down here fast. Kevin's house is on fire."

My great night was also going down in flames.

FIFTEEN

I helped Roz on with her coat, then whispered in her ear, "I've got to take a rain check. Emergency."

She turned to look at me for a few seconds then said, "Okay, we can get together again. It was a lovely evening."

We went out to the street and I hailed a cab for her. She kissed me on the cheek again and said, "Be careful. I definitely want a second date."

I smiled, said, "Me, too" and helped her into the cab, giving the driver a $20 bill after she told him her address. I watched her drive off.

I hailed a second cab and gave him Kevin's address.

The second half of the street was closed off by the fire department so the cabbie left me off 300 yards away. I ran down the block, as close as I could get. I saw Reilly's head towering above the local crowd that had gathered to watch and walked over to him.

He nodded to me and I shook my head. "How'd you know about it? Was it on the scanner?"

I knew he kept a police scanner on in his apartment for background noise.

"No, my new place is just back a block. I heard the sirens and came out to look. Place was already almost gone."

I swallowed hard. "Were they in there?"

He shook his head. "I don't know. I can't get close enough to ask anyone."

I scanned the firefighters, looking for a familiar face. I spotted Matt, a lieutenant with the New Haven fire department, standing near one of the engines, barking out directions.

I knew him a little from the Owl where he occasionally smoked cigars and always got hammered. I once sat and listened for an hour as he talked about his 42-foot fishing boat and what a money pit it was.

I walked over and raised my voice, trying hard to be heard over the noise. "Hey, Matt?"

He looked over, trying to focus on who was speaking to him, made the recognition but yelled that he couldn't talk just now.

I yelled back. "I understand but a friend lives here. Was there anybody in the house?"

He looked at me for a second and then came over.

"Tommy, right?" I nodded. "We have it under control. Burning for a good hour already. No, there doesn't seem to have been any one home. It's a two-family deal but evidently only one side was rented. Lots of shit, though. Basement especially, mattresses and that kind of stuff."

I looked at him with overwhelming relief. "Any idea how it started?"

He paused again and looked hard at me. Then he

continued, "I've seen a lot of these. From the speed of the burn and from the aromas inside, I'm pretty sure it was set. Just waiting on the SIS boys to get here to confirm." The Fire department has a special investigation team, just for these types of fires.

I thanked him and walked back over to Reilly. He was shaking a little from the cold and I suggested we go to his place to get warm.

It was an interesting apartment, a converted convent. Hardwood floors and lots of gates to go through. He had a first-floor apartment with a back staircase that he could smoke on. But he lit up as soon as we got in the door.

"Don't they give you shit if you smoke inside?" The neighborhood was becoming gentrified and everyone knew those people hated smoke of any kind. Smoke Nazis. The fire department would probably get complaints tomorrow about the smoke coming from Kevin's house.

"Fuck 'em. If I have to move again, I'll move again." He was still shaking. I wasn't sure if it was from the cold or from his ailments or from watching the fire.

I was shook up myself. "I think that fire was meant for me."

His head snapped towards me. "What? Whattya mean?"

I was trying to put it all together. "I mean, I dropped off Kevin's car and left the keys in the slot on the side, then went the back way to the street. If someone had been watching me, they would have thought I was still in the house."

He considered that. "Think it had anything to do with the car that was following you?"

I was starting to get angry. "We're looking at a case with a missing person that has arson at every turn and then this house goes up? That sound coincidental to you?"

I could see he was getting angry as well. "No, no, it doesn't."

"I think we need to ratchet this up a bit. I'm gonna make some phone calls tomorrow and see what I can find out about Callen. You're all set to go to the Register on Monday. I'm meeting the bartender from Diesel to see what she can tell me about the girl-friend. I think the Druids might be involved in this somehow, too. Know anyone with connections to them?"

The mention of the biker gang made him look at me funny and his head jerked back a little. "Really? Those guys are nasty fuckers. Why do you think they're involved?"

"Their name has been mentioned twice in the two days that I've been at this. And my limited knowledge of those guys is that they like setting fires. For hire."

He let that sink in. I could tell he was running through the rolodex in his head.

"I know an ex-member. Keeps a low profile. They don't like it when people leave the gang. Tend to get angry about it. He went underground for a few years but just started coming out to hang recently. I can call him."

I nodded. "Great. In the meantime, I need to get back to my place and make some calls. Can I grab a ride or should I call an Uber?"

He agreed to take me and we went outside and got in his old Audi. It smelled vaguely of leather, pot, fried food and Jameson. "You should bottle the smell in here. Make a fortune."

He laughed and drove me home, at top speed. He pulled up to the front of the building and I pondered for a second about a quick trip to the Owl but I really needed to make those phone calls, with Kevin being my first.

He revved the engine. "Get out. We'll talk tomorrow. Be careful."

It was the second time I'd heard that tonight but was too tired to fire off a clever retort and got out of the car and watched as he took off.

I went inside, thinking how quickly a day can change.

My first call was to Kevin. I decided not to mention my theory yet. It was supposition on my part and would just make him crazy. It rang six times before he picked up.

"What do you want?"

"Hey, it's me, Tommy. How are you doing?"

"How do you think I'm doing? The cops just called. We have no home, no stuff...my records are gone. A lot of that stuff is irreplaceable. The cops think it was set. Who would want to do this? It was a crappy old house. We were going to move eventually. Guess it's gonna be sooner rather than later. Thank god we were at the cabin for the weekend. The cops said there was no damage to the car, so I guess you dropped it off. Did you see anything? I cannot fucking believe this!"

I could tell that the adrenaline was coursing through him.

"No, I didn't see anything. Did you ever get the renter's insurance?" We had spoken about it a few months back. In that neighborhood, it was definitely a good idea.

"I did, I bought it after we talked. At least there's one thing that went right. I'm calling the guy on Monday and see what needs to be done. I'm guessin' we'll have to make a list of stuff we lost. I have to calm down first. My heart 's jumping out of my chest!"

I tried to calm him down. "I understand. Just take deep breaths and try to relax. Stuff can be replaced. The three of you are safe, that's all that matters."

We hung up after I said I would call him on Monday to see if there was anything I could help with. I felt guilty but I would have to get past it.

That was the tough one. I decided it was too late to make more calls. I was drained, emotionally and physically. The rest would wait. I checked all the locks and fell into bed, still dressed. I put my earbuds in to listen to music and dialed up Jaco Pastorius on my ancient iPod. A ridiculously fast run of bass notes started off "Donna Lee". It was the last thing I remembered.

SIXTEEN

I awoke the next morning around 7, made coffee and sat at the kitchen table to go over the last two days and yesterday in particular. My overwhelming feeling was the turning point came when I went out to Hamden to Miriam's house. Meeting Jack Callen and letting him put a face to a name. I couldn't prove anything but I felt it in my gut that was the source. But it may have been rumbling from hunger. I wanted to finish making the calls I had to make so I didn't want to go out to get breakfast. New Haven on Sunday was a "brunch" town, with restaurants serving overpriced Mimosas and runny poached eggs...but not until after 11. I decided to cook something myself, eat and work the phones.

I looked in the fridge and pulled out three eggs, some gruyere cheese and some heavy cream. I got my omelet pan off the wall and threw some butter in, turning on the heat. While I waited for it to get hot, I cracked the eggs into a bowl, added in some of the cream, beat the mixture briskly then poured it into the hot pan to make an omelet, adding the cheese in near the end. I ate it out of the pan between swigs of coffee.

I called Rosalind. It was still early but one of the many things she had said was that she was an early riser, even on her day off. She picked up after two rings.

"It's you. I'm so glad you called. Are you okay?" Caller ID. She had put my name into her phone. A good sign.

It felt good to hear her voice. "Yep, all good. No worries. Just wanted to say I had a great night and to apologize for the sudden end to it. I had your favorite wine here and my plan was that we would drink the entire bottle."

"And then?" She was being coy but it was a playful, sexy coy.

"And then we would open another."

She laughed, then got serious. "What happened? Was it anything to do with that awful fire down near Wooster Square? It's on the front page of the Register this morning. That poor family. Luckily, they were out of town. It could have been tragic."

The turn in the conversation brought the night before back into the front of my brain. I wasn't ready to go there yet.

"It actually was about that. The tenants are friends of mine. I talked to them last night. They're shaken up but, yeah, they're counting their blessings that they were out of town at this cabin they use upstate. Anyway, I wanted to say I had a lovely evening."

She didn't want to let it go. "The papers say it may have been arson. I can't believe what people do to each other these days..."

She paused and then continued. "Yes, I really had a lovely time. I love that restaurant. It was a special night that ended much too soon."

I was discovering that she could say things like that and sound so sexy, I wasn't sure I could stand it.

"We'll do it again soon. In the meantime, enjoy your Sunday and I'll call you during the week."

We hung up and I finished the remainder of the omelet. I took my time before I made the next call.

Mickey Dunn was a guy that I'd met a few years back when we were both doing mandatory community service work in the New Haven school system. I had gotten mine as a result of a beef I'd had in the Owl, when I'd hit a drunk for being rude to a lady friend I was with. His friends called the cops and I was arrested. It was a first offense and I was given probation and the community service to do. I also had to take an anger management class. It pissed me off.

Mickey was doing his for the same sort of reasons, after taking a bat to his wife's boyfriend's car when he found them cheating on him while he was out drinking. They'd come downtown, he spotted them and then went to town on the guy's new BMW. His connections kept him from doing harder time but the judge still needed to give him something so he was working the schools with me, talking to kids about learning to control one's temper. We both got a kick out of each other's speech to the kids and afterwards went and grabbed a coffee. We became friends. Sort of.

It was clear from the beginning that he was involved in a lot of stuff I didn't need to know about and my initial response was to stay clear of him, other than having the occasional drink or coffee. But he had insisted that he would be happy to help me if I needed anything so I called him.

He agreed to meet me across the street at the Owl at one o'clock. I read the Times, took another shower, watched a little of the CBS Sunday Morning program I'd recorded, then went across the street to meet him.

Mickey was already in the Owl went I went in. He had taken a seat all the way in the back, in one of the leather chairs they had up on a small stage, right in front of the big, walk-in humidor where they mixed the pipe tobacco and kept the extra boxes of cigars. It gave him a complete view of the bar. Hickok syndrome. There was live music here during the week, blues one night and jazz another, and they would take the chairs down and set up the bands on the stage. All other times, it was the quietest part of the place.

I walk the length of the bar and nodded at the Sunday regulars. Mike was a guy who did financial consulting and David worked for Amtrak. They were here every weekend. I'd sat with them a few times before, when the playoffs were on and seats were scarce. They were smart and funny and made those afternoons pass quickly. But I had no time to chat today.

Mickey was smoking a large cigar, some kind of Churchill. It was strong, if the aroma I caught as I drew close was an indication. He nodded at me and swept his left arm out, an indication for me to sit in the chair on left. I sat down and sank into the deep leather. It would be difficult to get up later.

We fell into our usual pattern that had developed in our other meetings. Somehow, I'd sensed that it was best for me to wait until he spoke first before I spoke. This time was no different.

Callie was working the floor instead of the bar and she came up and asked if I wanted anything. I ordered a cappuccino. She brought it two minutes later and I waited a minute for it to cool. After the first few sips, Mickey turned to me and asked, "Coffee? You on the wagon?"

I laughed and said no, just needed to be sharp today. He asked me why and I told him everything that had happened, from the first meeting with Miriam next door on Friday to the fire last night. I sipped a little between parts of the story for effect.

When I was done, Mickey mulled over everything I told him carefully. Another few minutes went by. I waited.

Finally, he turned to me and said, "You need to dump this case, this broad and the whole megillah. It's a bad beat." I'd always thought he sounded like he'd seen too many Bogart movies but today it seemed apropos, given the circumstances. I waited a little more.

"I don't know this Callen guy but I know some people who know him. He's out of Providence, Rhode Island, upwardly mobile, if you get what I mean. And nobody stands in his way. Had some issues there and moved here. No idea where the woman and her son fit in but dollars to donuts, he doesn't want anyone sniffing around as he starts this political campaign. The fire was a warning."

I looked at him. "They weren't trying to kill me?"

He laughed. "If they wanted you dead, you'd be dead. Too many questions would get asked. No, you were supposed to piss yourself and quit. It's not a bad idea. Quitting, not pissing yourself."

He didn't mince words. I thanked him for his time, got up and walked to the cash register in the front. I paid his tab and for my coffee, waved to the guys at their table, then walked out. It felt good to breathe some fresh air.

SEVENTEEN

I needed to clear my head and walk so I headed around the corner and went up Chapel Street. It was another nice day, with the sun trying to peek out from a mass of clouds. I had some time to kill so I stopped at Atticus Books, went in and browsed the mystery section. They had a pretty good bakery/deli so I bought a Pain Chocolat to eat later.

I turned up York Street, pausing to looking at the new construction going up there. More Yale housing. Just what the city needed. I walked to the corner and turned down Elm again, heading to Willoughby's to meet Amy.

I thought about what Mickey told me. I was actually a little nervous. This wasn't worth $250 a day. I made a mental note to ask her for more money when I saw Miriam again.

I walked to Willoughby's, on the corner of Church and Grove, where I said I would meet Amy. The shop had been there a long time, long before Starbucks came to town, before the myriad of other places. They used to have a second location on Chapel where they actually roasted the beans. It always smelled heavenly in there but, in those days, like sausage, people didn't want to see how their coffee was made. They closed after a year but kept this location. Just a bit ahead of their time was all.

It was just about 4:30 when I walked in and took the seat farthest from the door. The tables were close but this one had a little extra room around it. There was only one other person in the place, an older man reading the Sunday paper.

I draped my jacket across the chair and went to the counter to order. They made a killer hot chocolate here but I had the pastry from Atticus so I ordered a black coffee. The house brew was ultra-smooth, with no bitterness, and it would go with the silkiness of the pastry perfectly. The kid behind the counter pulled it from a large urn behind him and I took the nearly full porcelain cup back to my seat. The pastry was still warm and together with the hot coffee, I felt the comfort that a Sunday can bring.

I knew it would be short-lived.

Amy walked in around 4:55, spotted where I was sitting and came over. I gestured for her to sit but she looked around the shop first. The old man looked up from his paper but quickly went back to reading.

Secure that no one she knew was here, she sat down.

I asked if I could get her something but she shook her head no.

"I can't stay too long. My shift starts at 6 and I need to run an errand first." She seemed very nervous so I didn't waste any time.

"The other day, you intimated that there was more to the story than Dean told me. Tell me the real story."

"Dino. His name is Dino."

I could feel myself starting to scowl but tried to relax. "Okay, whatever, Dino. What Dino told me wasn't right? He said Marissa had been fired for dipping into the cash drawer."

She looked out the window. "Look, everyone who works there takes a few dollars every now and again. Marissa was no different. Dino pays shit. I actually think he may even be stealing our tips. And Marissa needed it more than any of us. Her boyfriend was a useless momma's boy who worked in a doughnut shop, for chrissakes. That one didn't fall far from the tree."

"Did David come into the bar a lot?"

She snorted. "He was there all the time. Especially once his mother moved in with that asshole."

"After his father died? After he had moved back in with his mother?"

She looked at me with disdain. "What are you talking about? He never lived anywhere except at home. Marissa was talking about them getting a place together but it never happened. They fought about it, a number of times, in the bar. She was getting tired of him being so namby-pamby. He had no balls. His mother made all the rules and he followed them to a T."

I sat back and thought about what she was saying. The woman I met at the Anchor and the woman she was describing seemed like complete opposites. My initial impression was that Miriam wouldn't say or do anything that her husband or boyfriend didn't tell her to do. But Amy made it sound like she had lied to me from the beginning.

She went on. "I know I said we weren't close but Marissa and I were actually good friends. She stayed at my house a lot of nights, especially when she felt threatened. She stayed over last week, just before she got fired but I haven't seen her since that night. I'm worried, about her and about the baby."

I had been writing in my notebook when she tossed that bombshell out. I looked at her.

"Marissa was pregnant?"

"10 weeks. But it wasn't David's."

"Was she seeing someone else?"

Amy looked the floor. You could tell this was painful for her.

"She saw my brother every now and then. His name is Tommy, too. But it wasn't a serious thing, I think she just wanted some laughs. I told her it was a mistake. My brother's wild, a real piece of work. Rides with the Druids."

My head was swimming with questions as I tried to put this together.

"You said she stayed at your place when she felt threatened... threatened by David?"

"No, are you kidding? David wouldn't say shit if he had a mouthful. No, by that jerk Callen. Guy had eight arms and liked to use them all. He was constantly hitting on Marissa. She was skeeved out by the guy but David would never stand up to him. The mother usually looked the other way, too. When Marissa told David she was pregnant, his first thought went to Callen. But it's my brother's kid. She never made it with Callen and I know Callen wouldn't force himself on her...not with Tommy in the picture. Callen did business with the Druids and Tommy would have killed him if he touched her and severed all ties."

It was a lot to take in. I was aware it was getting late for her and, as she stood up to leave, she had more to say.

"One last thing. It was a pretty nasty time when David's father died, especially under the circumstances. If you ask me, I don't think it was an accident. I think his parent's marriage was over and the mother was getting involved with his father's partner, Callen. I also think that David didn't think it was an accident. He'd get a few in him when he was at Diesel and said as much. I would bet that, if Callen got word that David suspected something and was making noise about it, or maybe had some evidence, something would happen to David. And maybe Marissa too. That's why I wanted to meet up with you. Hopefully, you can find them both but I really only care about finding Marissa and making sure she's okay."

She walked out of the coffee shop. I sat there for another 15 minutes, going over everything she told me. Wishing I had another pastry.

EIGHTEEN

I was hungry again and felt like I needed a pizza. Modern would do the trick. Modern always did the trick. I called Reilly and he agreed to meet me there, and he would bring along his sister Kathy. I left Willoughby's and walked down Grove to State Street, turned left and headed to Modern.

Modern was the third rung of the New Haven-style pizza wheel, the "Holy Trinity", although lots of locals (myself included) liked the pizza there more than any of the others in town. Modern had been in New Haven since 1934, in the same location. They made the thin crust pizza and served Foxon Park soda, made in East Haven, Ct. The perfect place to powwow.

Kathy and Seamus had walked over from his apartment. It was a solid 10-minute walk but they still beat me there and were sitting in one of the over-sized booths when I came in. They'd already ordered, knowing what I liked: Mozzarella and Bacon and Eggplant. There was a pitcher of cola on the table, a stack of napkins, paper plates and real forks. We were ready.

I kissed Kathy on the cheek. She was a handsome woman, a little older than Reilly but it was hard to tell from looking at her. She clearly liked the sun and would spend every moment on a beach if possible. I liked that she was here. She would give a new perspective to everything that happened without the cynicism Reilly and I usually brought to the party.

I brought her up to speed and then told them both what I had learned from Amy. By that time, the pizza arrived and we dug right in. I incurred Reilly's wrath by using my knife and fork to cut the points off so I could do the New Haven fold to eat the rest of my slices. He glared but I didn't care.

Kathy was intrigued by the whole story. She wanted to know more and asked me some pointed questions, which she also answered.

"Who has the most to lose in this scenario? I say it's Callen. And why? Because if any of this comes out, the fires, the kid, the bikers, the meth...his political career is over and he's looking at hard time. Makes you wonder what happened in Providence, no?"

Reilly and I looked at each other and we both nodded. I spoke first.

"I can go but I'll have to rent a car. Pretty sure I can't get Kevin's for a while. Kathy, that cop you dated is still in New Haven, yeah? Can you go down to the police station and see if there's anything new on the fire?"

She agreed. I looked at Reilly to try and read his expression but he was stone-faced. I kept going.

"You'll talk to your buddy that used to be in the

Druids, see what he can tell us?"

He stared hard at me then brought his hand down on the table, loudly. The other diners stared at us but he paid them no mind.

"Well, ya got me going to the Register to check the archives. Now ya want me to talk to another guy. You really need to drive all the way to Rhode Island?"

I understood that he was in a bad mood but I had already considered all the angles before I decided to go. "Yeah, I think so. Might be something there that will bring this thing into focus."

He looked away, angry.

Kathy cleared her throat. She had something to say. "You boys are forgetting how this whole thing started." She looked hard at me.

"Your original job was to find David. You're not getting any closer to that but you're willing to go on a wild goose chase to Rhode Island to dig in the past of a known criminal. Where's David and his girlfriend, that's what I'd be focused on." She seemed also angry. Siblings.

"So, you're pissed about something, too?"

She turned sharply and said, "Damn it, yes, I'm pissed. You're both playing with fire."

Reilly and I looked at each other and we both held it in as long as we possibly but then burst out laughing at the pun. Kathy finally joined in.

"You two are incorrigible."

I finally stopped laughing and looked at the two of them. "We should go have a drink, yeah?"

"Oi, frickin' Oi, lad." Respectful of his sister.

Reilly signaled the waitress to bring the check.

I paid the bill and we left for the Owl.

NINETEEN

I opened my eyes on Monday around 6:00 with a serious hangover, even with the two bottles of Poland Spring I drank before I went to sleep. Sunday night was a blur.

I showered and got dressed in a hurry, jeans and a black t-shirt, a blue sport coat and work boots. I had a long drive ahead of me and wasn't sure where the day would bring me, so I dressed down accordingly.

I went out the front, crossed the street, and went into Claire's for a carrot/cream cheese muffin and then up to Starbucks for an Americano. The Uber picked me up there and took me to the Hertz rental place near the train station. I filled out the paperwork and got into a new Nissan Maxima. Set the Bluetooth to my phone, dialed up Bill Evans' "Live at the Vanguard" then hit Interstate 95N for the two-hour drive to Providence.

I wasn't sure where I would start looking or begin asking questions but I had a lot of time to think about it. I finished the muffin before I was over the Q Bridge but sipped at the coffee until I was near Madison. There was another Starbucks there I liked so I stopped and got another Americano. I'm not sure the country runs on coffee but I certainly do.

I got to Providence around 9:30. I decided over the course of the drive that I would start at City Hall first and go from there. I had looked at a map and it was a short walk from there to the main headquarters of the police department. I doubted they'd tell me anything but an old sales rep one told me that if you don't A-S-K, you don't G-E-T. It was corny then, it was corny now, but occasionally it worked.

Finding City Hall was my first problem. Providence is a hodgepodge of one-way streets and I drove around for a while until I located it. Even my GPS was confused and I could swear that I heard the haughty woman whose voice the GPS used start to cry. I eventually pulled into the lot and a space marked "visitors" was open and waiting for me.

It was a very old building. A placard near the entrance said it was built in 1874 but you could tell by the smell of the place it had been around for some time.

I walked over to a window marked "information". There was an older woman working the desk. The sign said her name was Mildred Ryan. I gave her my name and asked if there was someone that I could talk to about Providence history, someone who could tell me where all the bodies were buried. She gave me a strange look so I smiled and asked who the City clerk was and if she could point me towards his office. She told me that office was currently vacant so I asked if there was somebody who knew the recent history of the city, one criminal in particular, and she directed me to Police headquarters, a five-minute walk.

I said, "Thanks, Millie!" left and strolled over.

When I got there, a younger, professional looking woman was waiting for me. Millie had evidently called ahead.

"Mr. Shore?"

"That would be me."

"My name is Rita Fenton. Millie phoned. You're looking for some information. Can you please follow me?" She was very precise.

We walked down a hallway to a small office. She went behind the desk and motioned for me to sit in the small leather chair in front of it. I looked around. A computer took up most of the desk, a few pictures, some reference books on shelves behind her, stacks of phone directories in a small bookcase. Not a lot going on.

"I'm the community liaison for the Providence Police department. Millie said you that had questions about someone with a criminal past you wanted to ask about?"

I laid it all out about Callen. I thought I could see her bristle when I said the name but I could have imagined it. I asked her if there was any way I could talk to someone who might know the history or background.

She turned towards the computer and began typing. I sat and watched her. Her expression never changed. After a few minutes, she turned back towards me.

"I'm sorry, Mr. Shore. Everything on Mr. Callen is classified. We can't help you."

I kept smiling. "Classified because he's public enemy #1 or classified because his records are protected?"

She kept looking straight at me, her facial expression remaining blank. "I'm sorry, but I really can't say. The records are classified."

It was clear no amount of charm would change her mind. There were rules and she obeyed them.

I thanked her, left her office and walked out the front door of police headquarters, ready to walk back to the rental car.

A black Mercedes pulled up to where I was standing. The back window went down and the man sitting back there behind the driver's side said, "Mr. Shore? Please get in."

It definitely wasn't a request. I looked at the driver and then back to the gentleman in the backseat. The driver kept his eyes straight ahead but I could see he had a gun in a shoulder holster under his jacket. I was weighing my options.

"My mother always told me not to get into cars with strange men."

The man in the back smiled. "Then let me introduce myself. I'm Robert Callen."

TWENTY

I looked closer and thought I could see a resemblance. I decided to take a chance. After all, I had my trusty blackjack in my back pocket. I got into the car and we started to cruise around Providence.

I put his age somewhere between 60 and 70. My first thought had been the father but maybe an uncle?

He wanted to make small talk first. "Do you know Providence, Mr. Shore?"

I had spent some time here when I was in the book business.

"The Convention Center a little. Ate a couple of good meals on Federal Hill. The Capital Grille used to be a favorite before they moved. Used to stay at the Westin. Spent a fair amount of time at Cigar Masters." A regular travelog.

He looked at me. "Ah, yes. I've spent a few lovely evenings there myself. It's a great place for meeting people and for making deals. The Westin is no longer there, though. It's an Omni now."

I was growing tired of this. "Well, it's certainly good that things change."

He nodded, missing the sarcasm. "It is indeed."

He paused and went on. I got the sense he was used to people listening to him when he spoke.

"So, I understand you're interested in finding out some information about my son. I'd like to help you but may I ask why you're inquiring?"

His son. I almost yelled "bingo" but held off. I decided to put most of my cards on the table.

"Mr. Callen, I'm from New Haven and I do some PI work occasionally. Last week, a woman asked me to find her 22-year old son. Turns out, the kid's father, a man named James Ross, had once been partners with your son in the real estate business. Until James died in a suspicious fire a few years ago and now your son is involved with the mother."

I paused. Hearing myself tell him the details out loud made me think it sounded like a soap opera. I continued.

"I met your son last weekend. Right after that, a friend's house went up in smoke. I believe it was because someone thought I'd be in there or as a warning to me to stop looking. I was also being followed by a car with Rhode Island plates. I'd heard that Jack had some trouble here a few years back and came up to see if I could get some more pieces to the puzzle. But I've hit a brick wall."

He took it all in.

"Yes. Here in Providence, we're quite protective of our own. I received a call from Rita very soon after you mentioned the Callen name."

He paused for effect.

"Mr. Shore, Rhode Island and Connecticut both have a storied past. While not exactly sister states, there has always been a relationship forged by both proximity and by mindset. This goes back to revolutionary days. Are you a reader of history, Mr. Shore?"

I wanted him to get comfortable talking. My gut said there were answers here.

"A little. Big picture stuff mainly. World wars and the like. Not much on local history. Watch the History Channel sometimes."

He looked at me and sighed.

"Those who do not learn from history are doomed to repeat it. I believe Santayana said that, or something like it. Do you agree, Mr. Shore?"

I shrugged and let him talk.

"Well, the two states had each other's backs back then. Rhode Island's first citizen, William Blackstone, had been forced out of Massachusetts and settled here. When war with the local Native American tribes broke out, Ct. fought with Rhode Island to defeat them. It is a very storied past."

I settled in for the story.

"Let me tell you about my history with New Haven. I used to do a lot of business with a man named Schiavone. Have you heard of him? He was a big part of renovating downtown New Haven back in the 80s. He saw a lot of possibility for New Haven as a stopping off point between New York and Boston for art, culture, music...and for people living there as a result of these things. He bought some hotels and other properties and set about realizing his vision. But it never really happened."

Callen was staring out the window on his side of the car, lost in his reminiscing. I kept quiet and listened.

"I was a financier back then and he came to me for funding. This man and I had a strong working relationship and I went to your city many times. I often brought Jack with me. He was a young man on the move back then, with lots of ambition.

"Jack fell in love with the city. I could never figure out why, except that he, too, saw the potential and for the money that could be made there.

"Then the craziness that the 90s turned into hit and hit hard. New Haven was still in the throes of urban decay from the previous decades and it had been an uphill battle. A few banks holding Schiavone's loans collapsed. We were having our own bank crisis here in Rhode Island. It was a mess."

He stopped talking and I could see him thinking back to that time in his mind. I sensed it was still painful for him. He went on.

"I had to pull my financing. Jack was devastated. We fought all the time. He finally decided to take matters into his own hands.

"I had a number of properties here that he ran for me. They were heavily insured. Jack knew a lot of people, including a lot of bad people. Unbeknownst to me, he formulated plans to destroy some of those properties, collect the insurance money, and funnel those funds back into New Haven."

There it was again. Arson. Almost every road I followed led back to it. I nodded encouragement for him to go on. "What happened?"

"He was careless and got caught. It was a mess. I did

everything in my power to make it go away and used up favors I'd spent years gathering. It kept him out of prison but he needed to leave Providence. It was a natural progression for him to move to New Haven. He met Mr. Ross and they had started a fairly successful real estate business. But when the next bank crisis came in 2008, they weren't able to ride it out and Ross ended up filing for bankruptcy. Jack fell back on his previous behaviors. It drove a wedge between us and ruined my relationship with my only son."

I had questions. "Why are you telling me all this? I'm a total stranger."

He looked at me. I thought he might have been tearing up a little.

"Mr. Shore, I'm old and I'm sick. I was hoping you might have had contact with my son and it seems you do, albeit tenuous. I was also hoping you could get a message to him. We've been estranged for quite some time. I've sent emissaries in the past but he's refused to see them."

There it was. Everybody wants something. It was to my advantage that it took a while to get to it. I proceeded carefully.

"I can probably do that. I need to go back to their house later today and could deliver a message."

"Thank you, Mr. Shore. I am very much in your debt."

We had circled around town and were back at City Hall, idling behind my car. I started to get out but stopped and twisted in the seat until I was looking at him directly.

"So, the message is...?"

It was as if a completely different man was sitting there. The hardness looking back at me was unnerving.

"He is not to run for Mayor. I don't need or want the publicity that comes with the vetting process or having certain authorities looking into his background and by association, mine. If he continues, there will be consequences. Please give that message to him. Someone from my office will be in touch."

I nodded. I couldn't get out of Providence fast enough.

TWENTY-ONE

I had a lot to think about on the ride home. The meeting with Callen the Elder had been enlightening but there were still a lot questions to be answered. The first being, where was I going to get lunch? I was hungry again.

I remembered a fish market in a little town called Flanders off Interstate 95. The market was also called Flanders. Not much imagination in the naming department but they also had a restaurant and made a killer fish and chips there. I decided to make the detour.

After the delicious late lunch, I felt like a nap but needed to get back to New Haven. I called Reilly from the car and left a message.

"It's me. On the way back from Providence. Lots to tell. Hope you made out at the Register. Call me back."

I hung up and hit the redial for Miriam Ross's number. She answered after one ring.

"Mr. Shore, where are you?" She sounded angry. Well, at least she had finally programmed my name into her phone.

I was purposely vague. "On the highway. Where

are you?" A good defense is a strong offense. It worked. She sounded confused.

"What do you mean, I'm home of course. You called me. And it's about time you did. I haven't heard from you since Saturday. Did you find anything out? Did you find David?"

I weighed my response, not sure how much to tell her. On the one hand, she was my client. She had paid me. There was a certain obligation there.

On the other hand, I wasn't sure what she could handle. I also had my doubts about her level of involvement. There was a lot of information to process about Jack Callen. Who knew how much he told her about his past?

Finally, I had no idea where David could be. Finding Marissa would help but she seemed to be in the wind as well. I had a nagging feeling that they were hiding out together.

I decided to stay vague.

"I didn't call you because I don't have much to report. David has gone underground and is doing a damn fine job of keeping a low profile. Every lead I follow has led to other leads that go nowhere. I still have a few I'm chasing down." Dazzle her with PI talk.

I heard her sigh. "Well, I paid you through tomorrow. If I don't hear from you by then, I want you to stop. You've already made my life difficult with Jack."

I changed the subject. Sort of. "How did the event go, the one you had catered?"

I could sense her mood change through the phone. It perked her up.

"Oh, it was splendid. A great time was had by all

and Jack raised a lot of the money he needs for the campaign."

Splendid. So much for parental concern. I wanted to wrap this conversation up.

"Listen, I'm on the highway driving and need to get off the phone but I'd like to speak to you in person next time. Is there a place we can meet?"

There was a twenty second silence and then she spoke. Back to being all business.

"I have to be in New Haven to settle up with Union League tomorrow. I have a 4:00 appointment until 5:00. Let's meet somewhere after that. If you've failed to do what I've asked you to do, I will need to terminate our services and alert the authorities. Agreed?"

I really didn't have a choice and said okay, hoping that I would find David between now and then, earn my money, and ride off into the sunset, a hero. But I knew the chances were slim. The kid and his girlfriend probably left town for whatever reasons, didn't tell Miriam, and she would hear from him in a month with "Hey Mom, doing fine in Florida" or someplace equally banal.

I agreed to meet her at the Union League Bar at 5:00 and hung up.

I drove into New Haven, turned in the car and walked back to my apartment. I took a shower, got dressed and checked my phone messages. There was a text from Reilly that he would meet me at the Owl after 6:00.

I locked up and walked across the street to wait for him.

TWENTY-TWO

Reilly's favorite seat was open so I sat in it. Although it was early, there were quite a few customers in the bar, mostly men. Almost all were sitting in the big leather chairs. Bill was working the bar and reading the Post. The only other person sitting at the bar was a guy I knew who owned a large funeral home on Wooster Square. I nodded at him as I sat down and he gave me a little wave. He'd sent some business my way in the past, mostly widows trying to recover pensions and the like. Bill would get a kick out of that.

I ordered a Sea Hag, an IPA that was made locally, and sipped it slowly while I waited. I ran everything over in my head. This was not a typical job for me. I had started doing this as a way to pick up extra cash after the divorce and between jobs. I'd spent a lot of years in the book business and read a lot of crime novels. Most of the people I knew read Faulkner or Steinbeck but I devoured Robert Parker and James Crumley, Raymond Chandler and John D. McDonald. When I needed to find extra income, I figured I could do what the heroes in those books did but until this case, the work had been about following cheating spouses or looking into domestic abuse cases. This one was closer to the stories in the novels I'd read and it was giving me pause. Still, I was invested in it and wanted to do the job I'd told Miriam I would do.

I wanted to shake the bad vibes I was getting. I looked at the Register that was on the bar to take my mind off stuff but my eyes immediately went to an article about a biker that had been found dead under the Forbes Bridge, near the Yale Boat House. Which was very near the bar that the Druids hung out in. He had been beaten so badly that he had yet to be identified but it was thought that he was either a member or an ex-member. I shook my head at the coincidence of hearing about these assholes yet again, showing up every which way I turned.

Reilly came in just as I finished reading it. He was clearly revved up and animated. He sat down on the corner seat next to me and started right in.

"Dude, the plot sickens. I went to the Register and this Callen guy is a real shit heel. He's had his hand in a ton of shady deals and a bunch of his properties went up in flames. The cops could never prove arson but every investigator that looked into them thought it was a real possibility."

He took a breath, motioned to Bill and ordered a gluten-free beer. When Bill put it down in front of him, he took a deep swig and went on.

"According to various reports in the papers, he's had his hand in different stuff all over New Haven. And get this... he hired David Ross to oversee a lot of them. The kid's name is on a bunch of the renovation permits. Jesus, Callen even owns the Taft."

That was a surprise. Again, there had been no mention of David's involvement from Miriam. The doubts I was having about her part in the whole thing were starting to grow, and I was thinking that she might be more involved than even I wanted to know. I told Reilly about the trip to Rhode Island, the meeting with Callen's father, and my conversation with Miriam. He slammed his hand on the bar.

"I say we go see the guy, get in his face, and make him confess. Bring along some muscle, like Tiny."

Tiny worked the door at the Owl on St. Patrick's Day and as a bouncer at some of the clubs around town. He was 6'4 and weighed over 300 pounds, mostly muscle. He was a gentle giant until he had to be something different.

I tried reasoning with him. It was a lost cause but I persisted.

"Look, Callen is definitely not the confessing type. He is the type that would have us hurt or killed. I think the key here is finding the kid and seeing where that takes us. Did Kathy talk to the cops about the fire at Kevin's house?"

He was overexcited and angry. This had become a big deal for him.

"She did. They're looking at it but nothing so far. They're not going to look that hard. No one got hurt and they're focused on other shit, rousting the homeless and setting up DUI stops." He had recently been stopped and just narrowly escaped a citation.

I pressed on. "Anything from your friend who used to run with the Druids?"

He glanced at me and then signaled Bill for another beer and two shots. I declined the shot he bought for me so he downed them both and continued talking. I ordered another Sea Hag.

"That's another thing. My friend who used to run with them said he knows this guy. Said Callen was hiring the Druids to do his shit work back when he ran with them. Says there were a number of guys that were down for anything, including setting fires and burning shit down. Callen even let them use some of his properties as meth labs. They'd set up shop in upscale neighborhoods where no one had a clue."

I stared at my beer. I was afraid of these guys. They had a reputation for violence and were a known source of drugs, guns and mayhem in the city. The cops had tried to shut them down a few times but they survived. The scuttlebutt was they were protected by someone on high.

I was at a loss for what to do. Reilly's plan was a bad one but I didn't have a better one. It was still early but I was tired from the drive and felt like I needed to sleep. I finished my beer and told him that I would call him tomorrow morning. I got up, went to the front register, paid the bill and walked out the door.

And froze in my tracks.

I was staring straight at the Taft, remembering what Reilly had just said: "Callen even owns the Taft."

It had been in front of me the entire time.

TWENTY-THREE

The Hotel Taft opened for business in 1912. William Howard Taft lived there for eight years after his presidency while he taught law at Yale. Presidents stayed there while campaigning. With the Shubert next door, it was the perfect place for famous and the infamous to gather, from the Marx Brothers and Al Jolson to Bogie and Spencer Tracy. Cole Porter wrote a song about it and Gary Trudeau featured it in Doonesbury. It made appearances in "All about Eve" and in "Splendor in the Grass"

In the twenties, during Prohibition, the owners opened the basement as a speakeasy. Once Prohibition ended, the owners converted the downstairs floor back to apartments but they were drafty and cold and management soon closed the floor off. But you could still get down there if you wanted.

I went in the front door and over to the elevator. You entered the building on the first floor but the elevator went down to what had become known locally as the "catacombs", a bevy of rooms below the ground floor. A series of hallways led you to the various apartments.

I got off the elevator, stopped and listened. I thought I could hear music playing, softly, down the corridor to the left. I followed that sound until I heard voices. A man and a woman, arguing in a stage whisper, trying to keep a low profile.

The door to the apartment was open slightly. I pushed on it and walked in.

David Ross and Marissa Grant were sitting at a makeshift table, drinking coffee. They froze when the saw me.

"Dr. Livingstone, I presume?"

They both looked at me like I was speaking another language. Education ain't what it used to be.

David spoke first. "Are you with the hotel? Look, I'm the property manager." He stood up. Going offensive to put someone off their game.

"Relax. I'm a private investigator your mother hired to find you. She's worried that you're in trouble." I paused. "Looks like you have the same worries."

I glanced around the place. I could see packages of food, enough for a few weeks, cans of tuna fish and bread, potato chips and peanut butter. Kid food.

There was a coffee maker on a counter, plugged into a socket along with a radio. There was a ratty mattress on the floor with a sheet bunched up on it. A few chairs around the improvised table. A couple of army-style duffel bags. There was also a funky smell in the air, like unwashed bodies after a week. Dust and filth were on everything, less so in the few areas they had been using.

I was taking it all in when I saw David move

towards one of the duffel bags. He grabbed out a gun and turned it towards me. I could see it was small caliber, a woman's pistol, a .22. I bet it belonged to Miriam.

"Stay where you are." David had clearly watched his share of cop shows on TV.

I laughed. "Does Miriam know you stole her gun?"

He took the bait. "I wouldn't know if she does. I haven't had contact with her in 10 days."

My first thought was what a sleuth I was. I stopped mentally patting myself on the back and focused on my next steps.

I looked at Marissa. She was crying. It threw me off. I wondered if she was there of her own free will. I turned back to David.

"Look, put that away. I'm on your side. My name is Tom Shore. Like I said, your mother asked me to find you. She just wants assurance you're okay. Nobody needs to know you're down here, okay?

He snickered. "Yeah, right, you're just going to tell her we're okay so that she can tell that psychopath so that he can send his biker goons to off us and torch the place? Not gonna happen."

I thought about what he was saying. He was so clearly scared that he would have had to have been very clever to concoct a lie like that off the top of his head. My feeling was he wasn't that savvy. I started getting those vibes about Miriam again and this was confirming those feelings. There was still a lot of unanswered questions. I tried a calm approach.

"How about you and I sit down and you tell me your side? I've met Callen and I've been looking into his background as a way to find you. I get it, he's a scumbag,

I get that. It wasn't until recently that I thought your mom knew more than she was letting on. You just confirmed that. Tell me your side."

I could see him deciding. It was confusing him. Marissa finally spoke.

"David, tell him what happened."

I could see him exhale, the pressure of making a decision off his shoulders. He had clearly led a sheltered life and wasn't used to being in charge. Marissa called the shots.

He used the gun to motion for me to sit in the spot he had been sitting in. I moved towards it slowly. I could take the gun away but I wanted his trust. He was making me very nervous, though.

"Sure, I'll sit but can you put the gun down or point it somewhere else? You're making me jumpy."

He lowered the .22 and walked behind Marissa, standing to her right. He began to tell the story, about his dad, about Callen, about their partnership, about the real estate business that went bad, about his dad dying in the fire. I had this information but I let him talk. It paid off.

"Not long after my dad died, I knew I needed to grow up and get more involved with the business. I went to my mother to discuss it. Callen was there. They decided that it was the right time to tell me that they had been having an affair, that Callen had bought out most of the business assets and that he and my mother were going to start living together...in our house! The balls on the guy!"

He was getting emotional and I could see him tearing up. Marissa put her hand on his arm and continued the story.

"Mr. Shore, David and I started seeing each other a few years back. I had a boyfriend before him that was a member of the Druids. You know who they are and what they're about?"

I nodded.

"Well, Jack had asked me to hook him up with them and I said I would. I told my ex, Bobby, and he put him in touch with Mason Rich, the MC President. Bobby told me they had done business together, bad business. Bobby was thinking about leaving the club."

She looked up at David and he was looking away. She went on.

"David and I split for a while and I hooked up with Bobby again. I got pregnant but Bobby didn't want to keep it. I did. David and I got together again and he told me he would raise the baby as if it were his and that he loved me."

She looked at him and smiled for the first time since I'd met them. He looked at her and I could see he'd been hit hard by the thunderbolt.

David took his turn.

"I needed to find a way to support a family. I took a job working for Jack, managing some of his properties. I still had another job. This place was one that I was overseeing. It's how I knew about the apartments down here."

He waited for me to respond. I nodded and said, "Uh-huh."

"Over time, I started to notice stuff. Callen would tell me to check out a building with a lot of issues, I'd do it and tell him, and nothing would be done about the issues. And then it would go up in smoke."

He paused for breath. "I also noticed that some of

the properties were being used by the Druids as meth labs. I started gathering evidence." Which accounted for the bottles Miriam found in his room.

He inhaled deeply. "When Jack and my mother were out one night, I went into the office at the house, my father's old office, and looked through some paperwork. I found this journal."

He rummaged around in the duffel again and pulled out a thick black ledger. He handed it to me and I looked through it. The first few pages looked legitimate, with listings for a number of the properties and any corresponding pertinent information.

About 20 pages in, I started to see listings with large red exes through them and a dollar figure written in the column next to it. Insurance payouts. I shook my head as it all came into focus.

"And Jack knows you have this?"

David swallowed hard. It was difficult for him to relay the story.

"I showed my mother first, to make her see what kind of man she was involved with. She swore she wouldn't tell Jack but wanted to think about what we should do next. She asked to keep the book but I insisted on keeping it in my possession."

He was starting to cry again. I finished the story for him. "Your mom told Callen."

He nodded and broke down. Marissa jumped in. "Callen came into David's room and he was pissed. I was staying over with David or I swear he would have killed David right then. He wanted the book but we had hidden it. He demanded we get it and we agreed but the first chance we had; we ran. Here."

I was running it over in my head. Something didn't

fit. Callen should have known to look for him at his properties. I asked them why he didn't. Marissa answered.

"David wrote his mother a letter, telling her that we were leaving town and that we needed cash. Bobby took it on his bike down to Philadelphia and mailed it, so the postmark would lead him to think we were on the road south. But when he came back..."

It was her turn to cry. I finished her sentence. "The Druids took him out."

She nodded. Bobby was the guy in the papers that had ended up dead. "Callen knew my history with Bobby. When he found out that he had helped us, Callen ordered him killed."

This simple case had turned deadly. I needed to think.

TWENTY-FOUR

I needed help. This thing was way out of my wheelhouse and I had no idea about what to do. I needed to make some calls but first had to assure these two I would help them.

"Listen. I need to talk to some people about Callen. Not the cops. But I can't fix this by myself. And you can't stay here. If I figured it out, he'll figure it out."

I stood up. I could see David fidgeting with the gun again, unsure that he could trust me. I ignored him and spoke to her.

"Look, I have a friend that can help. You can stay with him for a few days until I sort this out. You'll just have to trust me. Can you do that?"

She looked at David and he shrugged. She looked at me and said, "We don't seem to have a choice. We'll have to."

I nodded and said to David, "I need the gun."

He recoiled a bit and looked petulant. "Why?"

I told him I needed to go see his mother and Callen and that the gun would be my proof I saw the two of them. I also thought it may come in handy. I also told them that I was formulating a plan but that I would need a few days to pull it off.

They looked at each other, unsure. Then David handed me the .22. I pulled out my phone and dialed Reilly. He answered on the second ring.

"Hey, it's me. Where are you?"

He was still at the Owl. "Are you sober? Don't say anything. Pay your check, get your car and come to the parking spot in the alley on Temple, between Temple Grill and the hummus place. Keep it running and text me when you're there. I have the kid and his girlfriend. I need you to take them to your place and hide them for a few days. I'll make it worth your time."

He could tell from my voice it was serious so he said okay and hung up. I could always count on him when I needed to. I told David and Marissa that they were to pack only their essentials and get ready to leave immediately. They were shell-shocked but responded quickly to the order. They packed up the two duffel bags and were ready to go in 5 minutes. The book was under David's arm.

Now, for the real trust exercise. "David, I also need the book."

He balked hard at that one. "Not on your life. This is the only protection I have!"

I understood his reaction. But I needed it for leverage and I needed it as evidence.

"I understand how you feel. I'd be the same way. But it's a deal breaker. If you want out of this safely, I need to have it. You have my word that I will not double cross you."

He thought for a minute and once again turned to

Marissa. She took the book from him and handed it to me. She understood that there was no choice.

I led them out of the apartment and down a hall to a back entrance. We went up a flight of stairs. My memory was of an employee entrance back there that lead out to the courtyard. Hopefully, it would be unchained.

We got to the door but it wouldn't give easily. I stepped back and drove my heel into it, with all my weight behind it, and opened it enough for us to slip through.

I looked around to check if it was clear then motioned for them to follow. Reilly had texted me that he was already in the alley and the old Audi was there waiting. I got them into the back seat, threw the duffels in the trunk, told him I would call soon, and watched as they sped off for his apartment.

I went back up the alley to my place, changed clothing, made another phone call and took a cab back to the Hertz place. I rented a black Sonata and drove down State Street until the highway entrance and got on 95 towards Hamden. Once again, I hit redial and Miriam answered on the 2nd ring.

"Mr. Shore, where are you?"

I wasn't going to let her control this conversation. "Oh, goodie, you got me programmed."

She was not amused and said it again, "Where are you?" Louder this time.

I spoke back to her with as much hardness as I could put into my voice. "I'm on the way to your house. Is Callen there?"

She was surprised but recovered quickly. "He's

not... but he should be here shortly. Did you find David?"

I waited a few seconds and told her, "I did. We need to talk. I'll be there in 20 minutes," and hung up the phone.

My next call was to Providence.

TWENTY-FIVE

I got to the McMansion in twenty minutes and pulled in to the driveway. Both cars that had been there the last time were parked there again, along with the black Buick sedan that had been following me. I parked and went up the front walk. The door swung open before I stepped on the porch.

Miriam motioned for me to come in and then led me down a long hall to a large living room that held two enormous couches, two leather easy chairs and an oversized glass coffee table. It was a beautiful room, large and well appointed. There was a fireplace with a mirror over it that caught everything that was happening. I tried not to stare or fix my hair. Must be what they called the "sitting" room. There were book-cases on every wall but I glanced quickly and could see that the books were shelved by the color of the spine to form a pattern. Most likely they had never been read.

Callen was on the right side of the bigger couch that was facing the entrance to the room. In one of the leather chairs to his left sat a very thin man about 40, dressed in a black suit, cheap shoes and no tie.

My tail.

Miriam went over and sat on the same couch as Callen but on the opposite side.

Callen spoke first. "Mr. Shore, you've become quite the nuisance. Miriam insisted on hiring you so I've been patient. Do you have anything for us?"

The "us" rankled me, along with his demeanor. I ignored him and spoke directly to Miriam. "Mrs. Ross, is there somewhere more private where we can speak, maybe a 'Cone of Silence' room in the house?"

She remained quiet while Callen answered. "Ah yes, Miriam said you thought yourself to be quite the wit. But I don't really find you that funny, so please..."

I looked at Miriam and asked again, "No other room to talk in?"

I could see out of the corner of my eye that Callen was getting angry. Interrupting him while he was holding court was not something he was used to.

"Talk to me, Sir!" Both the volume and the pitch of his voice raised an octave.

I turned towards him. "Mrs. Ross is my client. I talk to her. If you want to discuss politics or baseball later, I can try and fit you in."

This time he smiled, but not with amusement. I could sense him seething underneath but he was trying to maintain a coolness.

I turned to the skinny guy and addressed the room. "And who's this, Ichabod Crane?"

Callen stood up quickly. "Mr. Ross, have you found David or not?!"

I looked at Miriam and she nodded for me to

answer, a look on her face that was both sad and plead-ing. She finally spoke.

"Please, Mr. Shore. Please tell us. I'm worried sick." Once again, I was getting mixed messages about her. Was she in on this or not? I spoke to the room but continued looking straight at her.

"Yes, I found him and I found Marissa. They're both safe but they're very scared. David thinks Jackie boy here is going to kill him. Or at least send someone to do it. He would never get his own hands dirty."

The stick man had gotten up and was standing in front of his chair. I had started to pull out the .22 to show Miriam my proof but as I did, I could see Callen's guy reaching into his pocket, pulling out a gun. Ichabod shot first and missed, hitting the mirror over the fire-place. The glass falling to the floor was muted by the carpet but it was still loud. I wondered if the seven years of bad luck belonged to him or me.

I turned and shot him in the meaty part of his thigh. Miriam's gun was a small caliber but a bullet from it can do some damage if it hits the right spot. He actually screamed, grabbed his leg, and when he did, I took two steps towards him and hit him in the temple with the butt of the .22. He went out immediately. I reached into his jacket and pulled out a chrome-plated .45.

Callen had remained in the place he had first stood up in. His mouth completely open, as if this outcome was totally unexpected. Miriam had begun to cry, softly.

"Mrs. Ross, I brought your gun with me to show you as proof I had seen David but also because I felt I would need it. I was right. David took it from your bedroom and had it for protection, which he felt he needed." I turned towards Callen, gun still in hand.

"Jack, sit down," I said, forcibly. He sat back on the couch.

I took out a page I had ripped from of the ledger and handed it to him. He knew what it was immediately. His head was down. I thought for a moment that he was holding in shame but knew better. He was just thinking about ways out. He looked up suddenly.

"Mr. Shore, I think you're a reasonable man. Give me a number. How much do you want? For the book and to walk away from this? How much would it take?"

I laughed. These guys were all the same. "What, and become Shake and Bake in a week or two? Nah, I'm good. Miriam paid me in advance for my time." I turned towards her. "Although, I may need a raise."

I looked back at Callen. I needed to buy some time. "Jack, your big mistake was underestimating me. You guys all think you know everything." I looked away from him and spoke directly to Miriam. "You're in over your head. This is not a good guy. This is a criminal who has committed fraud and arson and probably a whole lot more. I think he had James killed, most likely so he could use the business, and you, as a stepping stone to a political career."

Callen had gotten up again and shouted "Hey!" with feigned indignation. I was holding the gun in my left hand so I stepped over and threw a right hook, flush on his left cheek. He fell back onto the couch. I made a mental note to thank Ryan, my boxing trainer, and continued talking to Miriam.

"I think James was in on the arson at first but when Jack stepped it up, your husband didn't like it. He confronted Jack. Jack has a history of this kind of thing in Providence. He got rid of your husband and made some money in the process. I know about the affair. I think it was a long game plan on Jack's part to get you on his side, get rid of James, bring David into the business and then use David's clean background to acquire more property. The political thing fell into his lap. His ego got the better of him. He needed an upstanding wife to complete the picture."

I looked at her and could see she was trying to keep it under control but was losing that battle quickly. I turned towards Callen. He was holding his face with both hands. I went on.

"Jack, I went to Providence and met with your father. A very interesting man. He asked me to deliver a message to you that you were to stop with your political quest. That he doesn't like the spotlight that he knows would be put on him. But you forced my hand before I could talk to you.

"Which is why I called him on the way over here and told him the entire story and where you were living. And that I would be seeing you today. He seemed unhappier than before, which is saying something. He said he would be sending some fellas to visit."

As if on cue, I heard a car pull into the driveway. We could all hear three doors slam, almost in sync.

I looked over and could see Callen was scared.

"Jesus, man, what have you done?" The bite had gone out of his voice.

I looked at him and laughed. "What have I done? I did what needed to be done. You've ruined lives and property without concern for anyone but yourself. People died at whim. Now it's time to pay."

The doorbell rang and I told Miriam to let them in. I wasn't sure about her state of mind but she got up and went to let them in. I kept the gun trained on Callen until Miriam came back with three guys, all in black suits. I was ready to make a "Men in Black" comment but thought better of it.

The taller of the men asked Callen to come with him and Callen acquiesced immediately. He had seen this dance before. The tall guy handed me an envelope as he passed and told me it was from Mr. Callen. The Elder, I assumed. The other two grabbed the still unconscious Ichabod Crane and he started to come to. They put his arms around their shoulders and the five of them left the house. I went down the hall to the front window, saw them push Jack and Ichabod into the back seat, get in and take off.

Just like that.

I walked back down the hall to deal with Miriam.

TWENTY-SIX

Miriam and I moved to the kitchen. She offered me coffee and I accepted. Of course. It would give her something to do and I would have coffee. I could tell she needed to talk. She busied herself grinding beans, then put the grounds into a barista-worthy Italian coffee maker, only stopping to ask me if I needed cream or sugar. I shook my head and she went to another cupboard and pulled out imported biscotti. When she placed them on the table, I could see she was crying again. I tried to lighten the mood.

"No need for tears, biscotti will be fine."

She smiled but I could tell she was just humoring me. She finished making the coffee and poured us both a cup. I took a sip and marveled to myself at how delicious it was. Money may not buy happiness but it does buy amazing coffee.

She was quiet for a full five minutes and then the story began pouring out of her. How she had suspected Callen of being a bad guy but didn't know what to do after James died. How James had gotten so distant to her near the end and how she just needed to feel wanted and loved. How Jack came into her life at that time and how it "just happened". How after James died and Callen moved in, David got so angry and took up with Marissa. That she actually liked Marissa and wanted David to be happy but Jack never cared for David and only begrudgingly hired David to work for him. She now saw how that was part of his plan. How Jack always seemed to be more interested in Marissa.

I spoke up. "Marissa had an ex-boyfriend that was part of a motorcycle gang that did dirty work for Jack. In exchange, he let them use some of his dormant properties as meth labs. That was what you found in David's room. He was gathering evidence."

She looked at me and I could see her considering what I was telling her. She held her emotions in and went on.

"I wanted to go to the police after 3 days when David first went missing. Jack said no. I saw your ad in the Hamden Chronicle and he said okay to my contacting you. I think he thought that nothing would come of it, that you were fly-by-night. No offense."

I looked at her. "None taken." I should probably get a real license.

"Anyway, that Friday that I came downtown to see you was difficult for me. I had to put on a face the next day for the fund raiser. I really didn't have a lot of hope but thought you might find something that might give me some. When you came to the house, it surprised me. I thought then that you might actually find him. Jack was livid you came here. He made threats and sent Ronnie to tail you."

Ronnie. Must have been the skinny guy. Much better than Ichabod.

I had been nodding my head the entire time, tacitly urging her to tell her side of the story. Now it was my turn to talk.

I told her about Marissa and Diesel and about Bobby and Marissa. About the fire at Kevin's. About Providence. I told her she was going to be a grandmother. I left out who the father was. David could tell her or not tell her.

I was satisfied she was a victim here. Maybe not a completely innocent victim, but still a victim.

I called Reilly and a half hour later the old Audi pulled in the driveway. David and Marissa got out and Miriam could see she was with child. There was a lot of hugging and crying. I walked over to Reilly and we made plans to meet at the Owl the next day.

I drove home to my apartment, exhausted.

TWENTY-SEVEN

The next day, I took the Sonata back to the Hertz place and turned it in. The guy there told me I should get a monthly plan. I said he may be right and that I would consider it.

I walked up to my apartment. I was still quite tired. My hand hurt from hitting Callen.

I took another hot shower and relived the last four days over in my head. In retrospect, it had all fallen into place quickly but I had done a lot of leg work and the hot water went a long way towards washing the tired out of my system.

The envelope that Mr. Tall had handed me had five thousand dollars in cash in it. A gift from Callen the Elder that I was sure had strings tied to it that involved me not saying a word to anyone. I felt a quick tinge of remorse for dropping a dime on Jack but that passed quickly. The money would go a long way until the next case came along.

I got dressed and looked in the mirror. I was satisfied with what I saw. This had all worked out for the best. I had put a mother and son back together and brought down a really bad hombre in the mix.

I would worry about the Druids at a later date.

I walked out of the apartment and crossed over to the Owl to meet Reilly. He was already sitting in his seat.

"Oi, frickin', Oi. Nice job."

I looked at him. "Huh. A compliment...what have you done with Reilly?"

He chuckled appreciatively and said, "That was a fun one, eh? Kinda touch and go there for a minute. Whattya think happened to the ass wipe?"

I knew he meant Callen. "I have no idea. Maybe daddy sent him to his room without any supper." I had already put it behind me.

I gave Reilly $500 and bought a couple of great cigars. I opened up the wrapping on a My Father the Judge and straight cut the cap. I held my torch to it. Fire had its good applications. I pulled the smoke into my mouth and tasted notes of chocolate and ginger and spice. I exhaled and asked Reilly if he wanted one.

Reilly nodded that he did and then made his little motion with his thumb and pointer fingers to his lips, feigning a drinking motion. It meant he was ready for shots of Jameson.

I looked at him. He had come through in a big way and we both deserved a celebration.

I said, "Sure, I'll buy."

He looked at me like I had two heads. "You bet your arse you'll buy."

I sighed. Home.

EPILOGUE

I was sitting at my usual table in the Anchor when David Ross came in, looked around, spotted me and came over and sat down. It had been a month since he had been reunited with his mother and his confidence level had grown considerably.

I had been reading the Post and waiting on a corned beef sandwich. David signaled for the waitress but she ignored him.

"You gotta go over to the bar to order." He looked at me and said, "Never mind, I really can't stay, I just thought I'd get a club soda."

I looked at him. He was a different person that the one I had found hiding in the basement at the Taft. He told me he had taken over the business and could already see a huge turnaround, hoping it would happen in a year or two. That he and his mom were coming to terms with his father's death. And that they were both trying to put everything that went down behind them.

I said, "I'm happy for you," and I truly was. They'd had a rough patch there for a minute and both he,

Miriam and Marissa deserved a decent life. I asked after Marissa.

He beamed. "She's great. Getting bigger every day. We're due in November."

"That's great. And how about your mother? How's she holding up?"

The smile left his face and he looked down. "She's okay. It's going take some time but I think she'll be fine. She told me to send her best to you."

She would definitely be fine. She was stronger than she thought she was. "I'm glad I could help."

He stood there as if waiting to say something else. "Was there something more you needed from me?"

He had been holding a folder and opened it up and took out a newspaper clipping. It was from the Providence Journal. The clipping was an article about a fire that had occurred a week ago in an old abandoned building in East Providence. The building belonged to Robert Callen but had laid dormant for years. It made the news because the police had found two bodies in the ashes of the building. They couldn't identify them, even from dental records, and it was eventually thought by the authorities that they were two homeless men who had been squatting there and probably fell asleep with a lit cigarette.

David looked at me. "But then, we know better, right, Mr. Shore?"

I shrugged. Who the hell knows what goes on between a father and his son? Or a mother and son, for that matter.

David continued to look at me and waited for me to say something but I had nothing more to add. I shrugged again and he laughed.

"Thank you again, Mr. Shore. We owe you our lives."

He stood up. We shook hands and he walked out. As he did, Sally came over with my sandwich and asked, "Hey, didn't the kid wanna order something?"

I shook my head and she walked away. I tore into my sandwich. And when I was finished, there'd be a cigar and a coffee waiting next door at the Owl.

Man, I love this town.

PART 2

OLD HABITS

TWENTY-EIGHT

"How's your Burger?"

I was lost in reverie, looking out the front window of Caseus, from the corner table tucked just inside the restaurant. It was summer, a beautiful Tuesday in June, and the women of New Haven were dressed accordingly. Quite easy to get lost in thought.

I hadn't realized anyone was speaking to me. Meredith asked again, a little louder this time.

"Tommy. How's your burger?"

I turned and looked at her. This had always been my table whenever I ate here, which had been twice a week since they'd opened. Meredith almost always took care of me. Probably had to draw straws and, evidently, always lost. We would usually have a good conversation about a variety of subjects, from beekeeping to 70s pop songs, but today she was having a hard time breaking through my daydreaming.

"What? Oh, good, good, Meredith, as always. Good. Thanks."

She looked at me and shook her head. "Your mind is somewhere else today. I'll come back in a bit."

She was right. I was somewhere else.

It had been a few months since my last gig. Hiring out as a jack-of-all-trades cum private investigator, watching cheating spouses, looking into missing monies due widows from dead husbands...that's the kind of work I usually did. But two months ago I had gotten involved in something different.

I had been in the book business for many years when that industry caved in on itself. At 51 years old, I was a dinosaur without a place to go off to and go extinct in. Never really trained for anything, I had always been an avid reader of crime novels. While flailing around in search of the next steps to take in my brilliant career, it occurred to me at some point that I could do what the detectives and gumshoes in those books did. So I "hung out a shingle" and started advertising in the New Haven Register and all the surrounding local papers. I couldn't afford to get a real license so I kept my prices low enough that anyone looking for someone to do that kind of work at a low price wouldn't ask me for one.

In April, I had been sitting in the Anchor, a bar too conveniently located directly across the street from my apartment. They used to serve semi-decent food there and I went often. They'd since been purchased by a conglomerate, who turned it into a nightclub, rife with thump-thump music until all hours of the night. The nerve.

That Friday, I was eating lunch when a woman had walked into the bar and hired me to find her son. She looked like she had money and I was to be paid well for four days of work, well enough to pay the overdue rent on the sublet I was living in. I would also be able to afford some extras. Like food.

The case turned ugly almost immediately and involved some very nasty people out of Rhode Island. It ended up working out for the woman who hired me but I had made some serious enemies along the way, not the least of which was a local biker gang with their hands in drugs, extortion, violence for hire and arson.

They had made some threats. I sloughed most of it off but a backfire from a motorcycle parking in front of the Owl was enough to give me heart palpitations.

Nothing much had come my way since. I made some extra unexpected money by dropping dime on the bad guy in that case when his father paid me to let him know where he was... but there hadn't been a lot of business coming my way after that. Nothing was printed about it in the papers so no one from Hollywood just dying to make my story into a TV movie of the week came my way.

I picked at the fries that came with the burger. It was one of the best burgers in town but I wasn't hungry. Must be sick.

Caseus had opened in New Haven 10 years ago. Latin for "cheese", it was a fine cheese shop with a terrific restaurant wrapped around it. It had been top notch from the minute it opened. The owner, a young guy named Jason with an innate love of fromage, was a go-getter who loved new experiences. He ran the place as a family affair. His mom worked there, his brother worked there, and the staff felt like they were all part of making the place feel like home to customers. It had been managed by Megan for years, who ran a tight ship.

Meredith had also been there for a while, both in the cheese shop and in the restaurant. She knew what I liked and what I didn't like. She came back to check on me.

"What's up? Burger not cooked right?" I had left half on the plate. Very unusual for me.

"Nah, just thinking about other stuff. Not that hungry. Trying to figure out some things. How are you?"

She never let me get away with any misdirection and this time was no different.

"I'm fine but I'm a little worried about you. You're never not hungry."

I laughed. "Well, I might be starting an austerity diet soon. Money from the last case is drying up and unless I hit the lotto, I may need to get a real job. Whattya think, airline pilot or brain surgeon?"

She smiled. "Hey, who says you can't do both?" then took my glass away to bring me another Mexican coke. She always knew just what I needed.

I pulled out my phone to see if anyone had called me with a job since the last time I had looked, eight minutes ago. Nothing.

I called Reilly. He answered on two rings.

"Oi! What's shakin', Poirot?" I had a fleeting thought that this might have been a bad idea.

"Not much. Sitting in the window at Caseus, not eating lunch. Looking at the women of New Haven, feeling sorry for myself. What are you up to?"

"I'm working on a new canvas. Totally naked. A big one. Canvas, I mean. Eleven feet by eight feet. Gonna be amazing."

I reflected on the essence of that, trying desperately

to keep from getting a visual picture of the lanky Irishman sans clothes in my head, throwing paint at a canvas. His technique was founded in the punk scene and most of the stuff he'd done previously included taking a razor to the paintings once he felt they were close to being finished. Some of it was very cool, though.

"Sounds amazing. But at least you have that. I need something to occupy my mind. I need a case."

I heard him chuckle in the background. He tended to put the phone down and walk around when he talked to people. I thought I heard the slop of paint being thrown at a canvas.

"Hey! Hey!" I was yelling into my phone while trying to maintain some semblance of decorum in the restaurant. The other five tables around the bar were full with the lunch crowd from Yale. I got a couple of nasty looks. I nodded and smiled and waited. He finally picked up the receiver again.

"Sorry. Had a creative impulse that couldn't wait. Listen, I might have something. Do you remember Hugh, who I used to be friends with until he screwed me?"

I did remember him. He and Reilly were running buddies for a lot of years. Hugh would get involved with any kind of get-rich scheme that came down the pike - buying and selling gold coins, real estate, check cashing. I was sure he was all over Bitcoins now.

"Of course, I remember him. A major jerk-off. Lots of cockamamie schemes to make fast money. You two parted ways over one of them, right?"

I could hear him making adjustments to his canvas, which he typically strung across a contraption that looked like it came from the Inquisition. I tried to get him to focus.

"Yo!" Yelling rarely did the trick but there were few alternatives. He was back on the line. I was getting pissed.

"Do you think you can focus on one thing at a time, Sparky, like talking to me?"

He was amused. "Don't get your panties in a bunch, Hoss. I'm all yours."

I sighed. A conversation with him was never an easy thing.

"You were telling me about Hugh."

"Well, he used to live with that girl who worked at the Owl, Heather. You remember her, hippie chick, made her own soap, which she never used herself. Liked to drink and party."

I grunted and waited. A Reilly story could go on for hours.

He continued. "She's evidently in trouble. Got involved in a drug deal that went bad. Was buying weight from a guy out of West Haven to resell. She bought a bunch from him but then got ripped off when she went to sell it. Now the West Haven guy wants his dough which she doesn't have. She needs some time to get it together but she's afraid that West Haven guy won't give her the time. Wants somebody to act as the go-between and negotiate it."

I remembered that Heather was a major flake. She was nice enough but not the sharpest tool in the shed. It made perfect sense that she would get caught up in this kind of thing. Hugh would be an excellent teacher in the ways of illegitimate revenue.

"Where is this something for me? How do I get paid?"

It was a solid thirty seconds before Reilly answered. "Hugh is back in the picture. He's got cash. Wants to hire you to be the messenger. Says he'll pay a grand for you to just go and talk to the guy, let him know that she'll have the cash shortly. Reason with him."

I laughed out loud at that. Reason with him. What was I, Tom Hagan, sent to see the movie producer about Johnny Fontaine?

"I'm not sure I can do that. My limited knowledge of these kinds of people is that they don't usually respond to reason, that they want what they want when they want it and will do whatever they need to do to get it. What makes her think the guy will make a deal?"

Reilly had already checked out of our conversation. Someone had joined him in his apartment. I could hear female voices in the background and knew that my time for his attention was up. I hurried it along.

"Alright, listen, set up a meeting with Heather. But no Hugh. I'll talk to her alone, see what the real story is and make a decision. I need something quick but I want to be able to spend the money afterwards. I'll stop by in an hour or so."

He agreed. "Roger that. Later." And hung up.

I sat and looked out the window some more. I picked at the fries that had gone stone cold, hoping it wasn't a euphemism for what was to come.

TWENTY-NINE

I needed to walk. I finished my Coke, put money on the table, waved goodbye to Megan and Meredith, and left Caseus, turning left and heading down Trumbull Street. I took my time, admiring the great, old Victorian homes. Most of them now housed law firms or therapist offices. If you came to New Haven and saw only this street, you'd think the city was made up entirely of criminals and mental patients. Most days, you wouldn't be far off.

I passed Lincoln Street and turned to look right, towards the end of it. It was a short street that stopped at a building that used to be a movie house that had laid dormant for years. Once home to the Lincoln Theatre, they would play art films or feature clever double bills. Originally built in 1929, it was home to a number of theatrical groups until the mid-40s, after which it featured foreign films for Yale film students. Later, it became a second run movie house with a sense of humor. I saw "Mean Streets" paired with "Alice Doesn't Live Here Anymore" there, as well as "The

Wild Bunch" with "A Clockwork Orange". It closed in the early 80s. I missed it.

I took a slight dogleg to the right and walked until I hit State Street. I was taking my time, giving Reilly ample opportunity to deal with his guests and, if I was lucky, put on some clothes. It was a crapshoot what would greet me.

I walked up State and stopped to look at the menu of a new restaurant that had just recently opened, The Cast Iron Chef Chop House. I'd heard mixed things about it. The space it was in had been a steakhouse prior to this new one but had gone out of business. The hard money said New Haven couldn't sustain a high-end chop house but then two had opened in the last two months. Counting on alumni and well-off parents of Yale students to partake. Good luck. The menu seemed too big, like it was trying to be all things to all people. It would be interesting to see if it was there in a year.

This part of New Haven had a strange history. It had once been where the New Haven Arena stood, home to the New Haven Nighthawks hockey team, the Ringling Bros. circus when it came to town, and the only venue between NY and Boston for the major rock bands of the 60s and 70s. It came down in 1974, after the Coliseum was built. The FBI headquarters sat in that space now. Irony on a base level.

The city had been trying to gentrify the area for years but it never seemed to take. The ABC News affiliate building was here and there was a smattering of restaurants but most of the money ended up going farther down State Street.

I crossed State and walked over to Olive Street, crossing over Grand Avenue, passing Lucibello's Pastry shop. They had also been in New Haven since 1929, originally opened over on Chapel Street but then moved and had been in this location since the 50s. I wasn't a big fan of Italian pastry but I did love cannoli and they made the best in the city. I fought the urge to stop in and grab a dozen.

I turned down St. James and onto Hughes Place. Reilly lived in a converted convent about halfway down this street, deep in the heart of the Wooster Square neighborhood. Named for Revolutionary War General David Wooster, it had also been known as the Italian section of New Haven. Within a four-block area, there were six pizzerias, three pastry shops, a few Italian supermarkets and a number of good Italian restaurants. The streets were lined with cherry trees. It was a quick walk from downtown and every year they held a festival there to celebrate the Cherry blossoms. Thousands showed up.

I walked up the brick stairs to Reilly's apartment and rang his number on the board. It rang ten times and then hung up. I tried again and after the fifth ring, got buzzed in.

Reilly was in the middle of the room, staring at a canvas. He had put on a loose-fitting tank top and camouflage cargo pants and nothing else. There were two girls sitting on the floor, in various degrees of undress. Their faces were made up with unusual paint, smears of red and blue and dark eye shadow. He was alternating between throwing paint on the canvas and then picking up a camera and shooting pictures of the girls while he barked out the emotions he was seeking. Artists.

I sat at the long table next to the kitchen island and

watched. He had yet to acknowledge I was there. The girls seemed preoccupied as well. Or maybe stoned. It was anybody's guess.

After I minute, I started getting bored and cleared my throat, loudly. Reilly finally looked over.

"Oi, fuckin', Oi, how long have you been there?" I briefly wondered who had buzzed me in but thought better about asking.

"Just a few minutes. Did you set up the meeting with Heather?"

He looked over at the girls and tipped his head for them to leave. They got up and went downstairs, most likely to clean off the war paint and probably to wait for him to get rid of me. He turned back to me.

"I did. But Hugh says he has to be here. I told him that you said no, but he's insisting. Says it's his cash and that he wants to make sure you're clear on everything. They want to come here tonight, around midnight."

I stared at him. That was not how I wanted it to go.

"I'm not going to come here at midnight and meet Hugh. This is what I meant. He gets involved and it becomes a shit show. You should know that better than most."

He looked at me for a good thirty seconds. "Look, you need the job and the cash. He needs the favor. It's a match made in heaven. All that other shit is water under the bridge. He's going to pay me back what he owes me."

Ah, there it was.

Reilly could see I wasn't happy. He came over and put his arm around my shoulders. "Look, we'll hang at the Owl tonight until 11:30, come back over here, you'll hear him out and decide. You can say no. And if you turn into a pumpkin after midnight, I'll make sure you get back to your apartment."

He started cackling. Not a good look.

"Why can't he meet us at the Owl?" I already knew the answer.

"He got banned for life. Can't go in there without making a ruckus."

I got up and started out the door. He called after me. "Owl at 9:00?" I flipped him my middle finger then changed it to a thumbs up. He understood.

THIRTY

I left Reilly's and took the backstreets over to Chapel, crossed over State again and stopped in to the Elm City Co-op for a couple of bottles of Kevita Probiotic. I started drinking these after reading about the benefits it seemed to have on people with stomach issues. I was trying to be proactive with it but the only flavor I could tolerate was Lemon Cayenne. The co-op was the only place in town that carried it but they charged almost four bucks a bottle. Even though the store was a far piece from the highway, it still condoned robbery.

The store was a recent addition to the makeup of downtown. Lower Chapel had gone through some tough times since it's heyday in the 50s and 60s. It had once been the location of Goldie Libro's, one of the best music stores in the country, and Shartenberg's, a six-floor high, privately owned, department store. Now there was a Subway, a check cashing place, a few places to buy cheap jewelry and a Dunkin' Donuts.

I walked up Chapel, past the Starbucks and the Halel Guys, which had grown from a food cart into a restaurant.

Crossed Temple and went by another Dunkin' Donuts, another Subway, an ice cream shop and a running shoe store. I tried to poke my head into the Ordinary, a great bar that had opened a few years ago. It had been the dream of some Caseus alumni to open a high-end cocktail joint and this was the result. It was cool place to have a drink. When it was crowded, it was a horror show, as the space between the bar and the wall was very limited. Some pipes had burst during one of the excessively cold days in January and it was only recently reopened. An historical landmark space that required all kinds of rules and regulations to fix.

I turned the corner at College and thought briefly about having a cigar and a drink at the Owl, but I would be there later with Reilly and once a day was plenty. I entered my apartment in the Taft.

There was a handful of mail on the floor in front of my door. Flyers mostly. And an invitation to a party. I'd been seeing a woman for a few months and her kids were throwing her a birthday party. She must have asked them to invite me. It was to be held in the Union League, the site of our first real date together. I put it up on the refrigerator, using a magnet that said, "Drink Coffee Do Stupid Things Faster with More Energy" on it. It had been a gift from a friend who knew I had a major coffee problem.

I had a fair amount of time to kill before I went over to the Owl to meet Reilly. I thought about a nap, then quickly dismissed that notion. Warren Zevon's "I'll Sleep When I'm Dead" came into my head almost immediately. I made myself a silent promise to stay awake.

I did some busy work. Straightened out my office.

Aired the place out. Made the bed. Threw out old food, mostly Chinese take-out containers. Made it presentable in the off chance I would actually have someone to present it to.

Around 8:oo, I took a shower then threw on a blue Armani shirt, some black jeans and my trusty Hugo Boss black sport coat. I looked the part, if the part was a liquor salesman out to score. I took off the blazer and untucked my shirt. Casual. What all the PIs were wearing this season.

At a quarter to nine, I went over to the Owl. It was busy. They had live music on Tuesdays and the band was just setting up to play. The bar was full so I took a seat at one of the hi-tops near the cases that held boxes of cigars. My seat looked out at the bar and there was a basketball game on the TV over the bar. It was particularly smoky. Evidently, the state-of-the-art filtration system was on the fritz. Again.

Annie came over and asked me if I wanted a drink. She worked the weeknights and was a good kid, if a tad flaky. Wanted to be a model. Had posed for Reilly a few times. I wanted to stay sober.

"No, Annie, thanks. Just a club soda. But if you see Seamus, send him my way?"

She waved, said, "Will do" and headed towards the back, to the paying customers who tipped. It was anyone's bet that I would get the soda.

Reilly came in just at nine. He looked terrible, like the two "models" had put him through his paces. He sat down without saying a word and put his head on the table.

"Girls give you a workout?"

He looked up and glanced around the bar, looking for Annie. "I'm exhausted. I need a beer and a shot."

Annie came by as he said it and he placed the order. I reminded her about my club soda. Reilly lit a cig.

"Change of plans. Hugh's coming here."

I stopped short. "What? No, I'm not meeting him here. He can't come in here. What the fuck, Reilly?"

The big Irishman glared at me. "What's your problem? You need work, he's got work, end of story. Jeez, you'd think he was asking you to kill someone."

I shot him a glance. "Nice to see you're all buddy-buddy again. And all it took was for him to pay back a loan. Has he even paid you yet?"

He took his time answering. "No, not yet. Tonight. He's bringing your cash and mine."

I scoffed at that. "My cash against yours there's strings attached."

He didn't take the bet.

We sat and watched the game in silence for another ten minutes, until Reilly turned to me and said he was hungry. "Wanna eat? Chinks?"

I let the slur go. I realized I hadn't eaten since lunch so I agreed. We paid the check and walked down to Taste of China.

Taste of China was the best Chinese food in the city. Run by a family who had restaurants in Shanghai, there was an authenticity to every dish. We ordered a bunch of plates; Moo shu pork, dumplings, sizzling beef and shrimp, scallion pancakes, Ma La ribs and Yang Zhou fried rice. When it was over, we could barely move but our mood had changed and meeting Hugh was no longer a big deal. I paid the check and we waddled back to the Owl.

THIRTY-ONE

When Reilly and I returned, the bar was completely full and most of the tables were taken. We grabbed the table in the window when the people sitting there got up to leave and sat down to wait.

Hugh and Heather walked in around 11:15, with him leading the way and her a few steps behind. This had been their pattern since the beginning.

Hugh was tall, maybe six two. His hair was thinning but he still insisted on wearing it long, piled up into a modern version of what used to be known as a DA. A duck's ass. Appropriate.

He was all manic energy and loved making deals. He tended to speak very fast, used his hands to make a point, and would change from subject to subject without notice. It drove me crazy.

Heather was much more contained. She was almost as tall as Hugh but stooped over when she stood so she always seemed much shorter. She didn't say much. I wasn't sure if it was out of choice or if it was because she had no idea what was happening most of the time.

She affected a serious hippie vibe and I could usually smell the patchouli oil ten feet before she got to me.

I'd met them at a party Hugh threw in the big house that he and his then girlfriend Sara were renting in Stratford. Heather was a friend of Shannon's, one of the old bartenders at the Owl. Hugh frequented the Owl regularly in those days and invited them both to the party. About twenty minutes after Heather arrived, she and Hugh disappeared, returning just as the party was ending. Sara was visibly upset and there was a big fight. A week later, Hugh moved out of the Stratford house and into Heather's West Haven apartment.

I thought I'd heard the two had since parted ways and that Hugh had moved on to the next warm port in the storm. But evidently, they had reconciled, for whatever reasons. Now they were here.

Reilly got up and hugged Hugh and then Heather. "Hola! Long time, no see!"

I shot him a glance, wondering where the Reilly I knew had gone. I nodded at both of them, Heather first.

"What's up?"

They both sat down and Hugh tried to get the attention of Sarah, the other waitress. After thirty seconds, he gave up and said he'd go to the bar. "What's everyone want? I'm buying."

Reilly ordered a shot of Jameson and I nodded that I would have the same. He left and came back with the two shots and a double pour of cognac for him and Heather. Things had definitely gotten better for him.

I downed the shot and got down to business. "So, tell me what you need."

Hugh feigned surprise. "Jeez, no kiss first?"

I shrugged. "Been a long day. I wanna hear what

you've got and see if I can bring anything to the party. A boy needs his beauty sleep."

Hugh laughed. "I hear ya, I hear ya. Get to the point. I like that, actually. Too many people blah, blah, blah and never say what they want, ya know what I mean? They just go on and on and on. Ya know what I mean?"

I did know what he meant. I opened my hands to spur him on.

"And ...?"

He continued. "Heather has started a small business, supplying weed to people who need it medically but can't get their doctor to sign off on it. She's been using a guy in West Haven for her supply. He fronted her a bunch of his product, knowing she was good for it. We've done a lot business with him before. A lot of business."

I'd taken out my pad and a pen and started to write. I asked him the name of their supplier.

"He goes by White Clarence."

I looked up and smirked. "Is there a Black Clarence as well?"

Hugh looked at me in a way he thought was hard.

"Oh yeah, I forgot, you're quite the comic. As a matter of fact, there was a 'Black Clarence' but he passed. Tragically, I might add."

I sneered at the way he said it, like he was somehow involved. He always wanted to be a badass, but fell short in the cojones department. I turned towards Heather.

"So, what happened?"

She started to talk and Hugh interrupted. "She got ripped off, is what happened. Client was new and had a gun and took everything she had. Everything. Entire stash she had in her car."

I hadn't turned away from looking at Heather but did now. "It's been awhile since I've seen either of you. Does she still have the ability to talk?"

I could see Hugh get irritated and start to answer but Heather put her hand on his to stop him.

"Yes, I can talk."

I turned back to her. "Welcome to the Owl. Maybe I can hear your version of this?"

I got more than I bargained for. She started to tell me her story, and weeks of pent up information came pouring out. About clients, about prices, about buying "stock" from White Clarence, about keeping the entire stash in her car because she didn't trust the neighborhood where they lived.

I asked her how much she owed this guy.

"Thirteen Grand." Without blinking an eye.

I was pretty sure my eyes were blinking. "How did you get to that number? That's a shitload of weed. He gave you that much credit?"

She hung her head then looked at Hugh. "Well, some of it is vig."

Ah, that made sense. They were being squeezed. "How much is the original debt?"

"Nine Grand." Hugh had answered then put up both his hands up to indicate he wouldn't say any more.

Heather continued. "It's five hundred a day in interest. It's been a week. Today is day eight."

She started to cry. Hugh moved quickly and put his arm around her. It didn't seem like he was actually comforting her. I got the sense there was more story here. And I was getting bored.

"So, you want me to go meet with White Clarence and offer him what, that you can pay him back? When?"

Hugh jumped in again. "Look, I'll pay you a grand to go meet with the guy and ask him to give us some grace time, a week, maybe two. I can pay him back but I can't keep up with the vig. I've got a few things working and my capital is tied up there. But, if everything works out, I'll have all his money and a reasonable amount of interest for him by then, Three weeks, tops. Offer him ten Grand."

I laughed. I repeated to them that my limited knowledge of guys like White Clarence told me that this was a futile endeavor, that he wouldn't make this kind of deal. But I was intrigued as well. There was definitely more to this.

I got a few more details. They actually had a cell phone number for the guy. The new world of crime. No matter how bad you are, stay accessible and connected. Hugh gave me an envelope with 20 fifties in it. I counted it and could see him getting irritated but he kept his mouth shut. I told them I would call their guy and set up a meet, then got up to leave. Heather jumped up and hugged me. I shook my head. Great, now it would take hours for the smell of patchouli to fade away.

THIRTY-TWO

I walked out of the Owl and started across the street, trying to shake off the aroma. I didn't notice the unmarked cop car parked in front of my building.

The two plainclothes got out just as I stepped onto the sidewalk from the street and stood in front of me. One was overweight who probably described himself as "burly". The other was shorter but dressed better. A lot better.

The Armani model flipped open a badge while the burly guy opened the back door of the Ford. I stopped short and didn't look at the badge.

"Gents, really, I know I just jaywalked there but I live right here, in this building."

Burly guy spoke first. "Get in." It wasn't a request. I got in the backseat and he slammed the door.

Burly guy then went around and got in the front passenger seat while Armani guy waited outside.

He didn't turn around to look at me, just started talking.

"We're with the DEA, Mr. Shore. My name's John

Macklin and my partner is Bill Pete. We've been part of a team that's been looking into the Druids. For a while now. We were hoping that you might have some information that you would want to share with us."

I thought about the Druids. I had recently been involved with them, although not directly. They had an affiliation with the bad guys in my missing person case. When I brought those bad guys down, I interrupted a steady stream of income for the Druids. Word was the gang wasn't happy. I'd imagined some run-ins with them but nothing overt had happened yet. They just always seemed to be nearby. A few even frequented the Owl even though they had their own bar near East Haven.

I was trying to process what was going on when Macklin turned towards me and raised his voice.

"Shore? You're daydreaming. Focus on what I'm asking. Anything you can tell me, anything at all? These are nasty pricks. Your name has come up on more than a few phone conversations."

I jerked my head up at that piece of information, a cold chill of fear coming over me.

"Like how? What are they saying?"

Macklin could see he'd touched a nerve. He backed down a little.

"Mostly that they weren't happy with what happened with that Callen guy, that there was more attention being paid to them by the local cops, that maybe you were to blame. Fill me in."

I told him the whole story. About Providence and the Callens. About the fires. About finding the kid and his girlfriend. About what may have happened to Jack and his bodyguard after it was over.

He listened without saying a word. When I was done, he sat for a minute, got out his wallet and gave me his card.

"Look, anything comes up, call me first. Anything. You don't need to be a big shot here. These assholes are dangerous and don't screw around."

I nodded. "Can I go?"

He leaned over and knocked on the driver side window and his partner opened the back door to let me out. But he couldn't resist.

"And Shore? Next time, go a little easier on the patchouli."

I walked into my apartment building. I couldn't get in the shower fast enough.

After that, I got in to bed and picked up Dostoyevsky's Notes from the Underground. I had vowed to myself that I would read it. I was asleep ten pages in.

THIRTY-THREE

I woke up at 9 the next morning with a terrible headache. I didn't think that I had that much to drink last night so I laid there, thinking that the stress of the day had caused it. A day that started off with pretty girls and sunshine and cheeseburgers but ended with ominous clouds, DEA agents and patchouli oil. I decided to get up and vowed never to read another depressing novel at bedtime again.

I showered again (just to be sure), then toasted a bagel I'd bought at the deli on Crown Street. I was out of cream cheese so I took out some Irish butter, zapped it for 20 seconds, and slathered it on the bagel. My coffee finished brewing so I poured a cup and sat down to read the Register.

The New Haven Register had gotten progressively smaller and more expensive over the last few years. I'd gotten into an old guy thing of checking the obits first to see if I was in there. If I wasn't, I skimmed the rest. Aside from the ads and the sports pages, there wasn't a lot to read in it.

When I was done, I looked at the clock on the stove and saw it was almost 10:30. Might just be a respectable time for a drug dealer to be awake and open for business. I got out the number Heather had given me and dialed. No answer.

I tried 3 more times. On the third attempt, a guy picked up. "Talk."

Great, another charm school grad.

"I'm looking for White Clarence."

I heard shuffling in the background.

"Who askin'?"

"My name is Tommy Shore. I represent certain business associates of his."

Keep it professional.

"Represent? Like a lawyer?"

I needed to nip the twenty questions shit in the bud.

Making my voice hard, I said, "Like an agent. Is he there? If he's not there, tell him to call the number that came up," and hung up. I waited for 2 minutes and my phone rang.

"This is Clarence. Who this?"

I wanted the upper hand back. "White Clarence or Black Clarence?"

A pause. "White. Black's dead."

I told him who I was and who I represented. He was skeptical at first but we agreed to meet in a public place. There was a restaurant in West Haven by the water called Jimmie's that catered to the elderly and the obese. We would meet there tonight at 6:00, dinner time, when it would be crowded. He told me to come alone and that he would do the same. I hung up first before he could ask more questions.

I called Reilly, even though it was early. He picked up after 8 rings. "What?"

"It's T. Where are you?"

"Where do you think I am, I'm working in Fairfield, checking out a $3 million dollar dump."

Reilly had a successful inspection business down along the Gold Coast, from Fairfield to Greenwich and north. He was always crawling around spaces in multi-million dollar homes. He called nearly all of them dumps.

"How about I buy you dinner tonight? I set it up to meet the pot guy at Jimmie's. I need a ride and I'd like some back up. You can get those fried clams you love." Reilly watching my back was not a perfect solution but my choices here were limited.

There was a pause, then "Sure. What time?"

"We agreed on 6:00 but pick me up at 4:30. I want to scout the place out a bit before we go in."

He grunted. "Oi." Then hung up.

"A man of few words," I said out loud and then shook my head when I realized that I was talking to myself. Maybe I needed a dog. I dialed Heather's cell. She picked up on the first ring.

"Tommy, I was hoping you'd call. I want to apologize for Hugh last night, he gets..."

I stopped her. "No worries. It's fine. I'm doing this for you. I spoke to your guy. We're meeting tonight."

I could hear her struggle to catch a breath. "Thank you, Tommy, thank you. I'm sick over this thing. Hugh is pissed and he's been horrible about it."

That gave me pause. I seemed to remember some domestic squabbles that ended in 911 calls. I just couldn't remember who the aggressor was. There may have been a little light S&M to boot.

"You're okay? Things aren't getting out of hand, so to speak?"

She chuckled. "No, it's all good. Let us know what you find out. And Tommy...." she paused to make sure she had my attention.

"Yeah?"

"Tread lightly. These guys may seem half-assed to you but they're crazy. And they're playing out some badass drug kingpin fantasy. Don't not take them seriously."

I told her I wouldn't and didn't even correct the grammar. Guess I was finally maturing.

THIRTY-FOUR

I killed the rest of the afternoon at the Owl. It was a great place to let time pass. What had once been a very good cigar store where the hoi polloi of old New Haven bought their cigars was now a place to kick back and while away the day. It had changed about 12 years back, when the owners added a bar. It still had pretensions of being a high-end establishment but the clientele had changed constantly and dramatically. At night, it could be a raucous pick up joint with smoke, but during the day it was a calm place to sit, sip a great coffee and enjoy a fine cigar. There was always a handful of regulars in there and I usually had good conversations about New Haven restaurants or about the changes the city was going through. Today was no different. The afternoon disappeared quickly.

Reilly picked me up exactly at 4:30. He looked terrible and his first words were, "I'm exhausted." This was a typical greeting so I didn't pay much attention.

He continued. "95 was a bear, fuckin' trucks all over the road...and the construction. I don't think they'll ever finish it. They fix one section and then start immediately on another. No wonder the state has no goddamn money!"

It was a lament I'd heard before and I chalked it up to the price of the ride. After a while, he clammed up.

We went up Frontage Road until the end, then turned left to go up Ella Grasso Boulevard and over to Campbell Avenue.

West Haven was basically a blue-collar, middle-class bedroom community of New Haven. The city had suffered through financial problems since the 1990s and many of the areas we passed were a reflection of those problems. We went by the University of New Haven but it wasn't doing a lot to bring up the tenor of the neighborhoods.

Campbell Avenue ended at the beach. What was once a thriving tourist attraction along the lines of Coney Island was now a bevy of strip malls and hi-rise apartments. Mediocre restaurants dotted the landscape, with many of the good ones shuttered.

Jimmie's Restaurant was set back, nearer the beach. It had once been a thriving fast- food hot dog stand, before there was the fast food we now knew. Families would come there in droves, park, get in line, order at one window, pick up at another, then go back to their car or sit on a bench and eat. When they were done, they'd throw the trash out the window or on the ground. Three times a day, a giant street sweeper would traverse the lot, picking up the discarded trash, while hundreds of seagulls hovered above, looking for garbage. When they paved it over and moved further down the beach, the seagulls still flew over, looking for something to eat based on their sense memory. A different time.

It had only taken us a half hour to get here. I had Reilly drive around the lot to see if there was anything suspicious. These kind of wannabe gangsters tended to favor large SUVs, Escalades or Expeditions. It was clear but it was also early. We found a space in a nearby strip mall where we could watch the Jimmie's lot, in front of a nail salon. We sat there for 30 minutes before Reilly spoke.

"So, just what do you think you're gonna say to these mutts? I doubt they're gonna be understanding business guys, open to negotiation. This could be dangerous."

I was looking out the window, watching the lot. I turned to look at him, incredulous that he was bringing this up now.

"You were there when I said I would do this. You fronted the thing from the start. NOW you're having second thoughts?"

He wouldn't answer or meet my gaze, just kept staring out the window. After a minute, he said, "I'm hungry. I didn't eat today."

I was aware that I was rolling my eyes but forced myself to stop. I knew he was not feeling great.

"Okay, drive back over to the lot and park over on the far left. They opened at 5:30. We can go in and eat and watch the door for when they arrive."

He fired up the Audi and we zipped across the parking lot and into a space close to the back exit.

"Just in case." If nothing else, he was cautious.

We walked into the restaurant and had to shield our eyes from the brightness of the lights. The hostess, pretty, maybe 25 years old, noticed our wincing and laughed.

"We get a lot of elderly customers. They need it to be bright in here. Sometimes I think I should wear sunglasses. Two?"

I pointed and asked for a booth in the middle of the older folks that had been there since 5:31. She shot me a funny look but took me over to a booth that was fairly well hidden from most of the restaurant but where we could still see the door and most of the tables.

"How's this?" It was exactly where I had pointed.

"Terrific. Thanks. Can I get a Coke and an Omission for my friend?"

She looked at me funny and said she would send over a waitress. How presumptive of me to think she would take a drink order.

Our waitress came over and we ordered drinks, a whole belly clam plate for Reilly and a lobster roll for me. The food here came in piles that were bigger than your head and almost everyone left with a doggie bag. Nothing like coagulated fried food the next day.

At five minutes to 6:00, six very large men came in. Their ages ranged from early twenties to early thirties and they all wore a kind of uniform - Grey sweats, a Carhartt t-shirt in varying colors, a loose-fitting Tommy Hilfiger jacket and blond Timberlands. Three of the posse were black and three were white. Diversity.

We watched as three of them went to a rounded booth away from the crowd but near the windows, overlooking the ocean. The other three went to a booth near that one. Bodyguards.

So much for coming alone.

THIRTY-FIVE

Our food had come quickly but I wasn't really hungry so I picked at the lobster meat and a few fries.

When the Backstreet Boys had come in, I had pushed my plate away, waiting for them to be seated.

I told Reilly that I was going over.

I approached the three at the back table, the one I thought had White Clarence sitting in the middle. They were studying their menus like there was going to be a quiz afterwards. As I got closer, I could see that all three were members of the 300-pound club. Meeting at Jimmie's now made much more sense.

They looked at me as I approached and out of the corner of my eye, I could see the guys at the other booth shift their weight and reach their hands into their jackets.

The big guy in the middle put a hand up. I noticed he never dropped the menu. The guys at the other table relaxed. The two mutts sitting with Clarence did the same.

"White Clarence, I presume?"

He looked at me for a good 20 seconds before answering.

"That would be me. Who's askin'?"

This was going to be a long meeting.

"I'm Tommy Shore. I'm here on behalf of Heather and Hugh."

Clarence laughed, a guttural forced kind of laugh. He addressed his dinner mates.

"Huh. They gotta send over a representative. They gotta send a negotiator. Tell me, am I that difficult to get along with, that they gotta send someone along to ask me for sumthin'? I'm a reasonable guy, no?"

The other two at the table nodded but didn't answer. My first thought was they would have difficulty speaking in full sentences but then I realized they were probably scared of this guy. I focused all my attention on Clarence.

"I'd like a minute of your time to speak with you, if that's okay?"

Kill 'em with feigned politeness and faux respect. It usually worked.

"See that. Respect. I like that. Sit down, Mr. Shore. Jimmy, move your ass over to that other booth."

Booyah.

The one closest to me got up. He towered over me and I could hear him grunt a little as he moved over to the other table. I sat where he had been sitting.

Clarence looked at the menu again then put it down on the table.

"I don't know why we even get a menu; we always order the same shit." He laughed and waved the waitress over. She had been nervously hovering near the drink station.

"The usual, honey, and Cokes all around. Coke, Mr. Shore?"

I held up my hand to say no but he ignored it and told her to bring me one. She left and he called out after her, "And lots of lemons!" They were clearly regulars here.

He turned to me and got a serious look on his face. "So, talk."

I had been rehearsing what to say in my head. Sitting at the table now, it all seemed trite. But I had taken the money from Hugh, so I gave it my best shot.

"My understanding is that they bought some product from you, with the expectation that they would be able to pay you for it quickly. Due to unforeseen circumstances, there's been a delay in their ability to pay it back. They're having trouble getting the funds together, as it's tied up in other ventures. The interest is killing them. $4000 on top of the original nine they borrowed in goods."

Clarence held a finger up. "$4500. Today is another day."

I looked to see if he was taking this serious or just humoring me but I couldn't read him.

"Right, $4500. What Hugh and Heather would like me to ask you for is more time, without the vig. They can get you $10 grand within a week. They also want to buy more product to replace the product they lost. On credit, of course, but with the promise that they will have all your money for you very quickly. They have buyers. They need materials."

He pondered the offer.

"So, let me get this straight. You want me to forego $3500 dollars in order to give them time to pay me less than they owe me, and then borrow more? Don't sound like much of a deal to me, sound good to you? "

He was looking at his other guy at the table, who shook his head no.

I knew I needed to give him a simple reason. This could go wrong easily. I decided to play to his business acumen and hope there was some. I could sense he wasn't a fan of Hugh's so I would keep him out of the equation.

"Look, any business model worth its salt knows that you need consumers to be successful in the long run. Heather is your consumer. She has her consumers. It's a good arrangement. The way it stands now is short term thinking. You could have her as a partner for a while. And make a lot of money."

He continued to stare at me for a few minutes, as if in a trance. I assumed he was weighing his options. Or my options.

His reverie was interrupted by the waitress, delivering plates of heaping mounds of food. She had to enlist another server to bring the drinks. I was fascinated and would have liked to have watched them eat it all, like one would be watching an anaconda eating a goat. But I wanted out of there more.

"Whattya think? Can I go back to them and tell them you're a reasonable man and business partner and they have the time they need?"

Clarence looked at me then waved the back of his hand for me to go, like the Pharaoh dismissing Moses.

"Get outta here. They have the time they want. But

tell them that if I don't have my money and new orders for product in a week, I'm gonna visit them. And you."

I nodded at him and got up. Nobody looked up from their food this time, just dug in with gusto. Made me wish I had gone into the bathroom to see if Clemenza had done his job.

THIRTY-SIX

I went over to Reilly and beckoned to him that we needed to leave immediately. He had finished his clams and was picking on my fries. I threw 3 twenties on the table and hoped that would cover it. He grabbed a handful of fries for the road then got up and we walked out the door to go to the car.

"How'd it go?"

I wanted to get out before Clarence had a change of heart. "I'll tell you in the car."

Reilly had gotten the keys out of his leather jacket and tossed them to me. There was French fry grease on them. "Okay, but you gotta drive. I can't see at night."

I'd forgotten about his night blindness. It was only dusk but he wouldn't take the chance. I hit the button and unlocked the Audi doors. We got in and headed back to New Haven. The highway would still be jammed at this hour so I opted for going over the side streets. I went by the ocean front. It had once been home to a few good restaurants and drive-ins but time had not been kind to the area. Almost all were shuttered and the few open had very few cars parked outside. But it was a great view.

Reilly snickered. "What are we, on a date?"

I shot him a glance. "You're not my type. I just like this view at this time of day. You want me to describe it to you?"

He sneered. "Funny stuff. We pass the sewage treatment plant? That always stirs the loins."

He paused, bored with the back and forth. "So, tell me what happened."

I told him about the conversation and didn't leave anything out. I could tell he was disgusted.

"Fat, frickin' wannabe gangsters. Ass wipes. The balls on these guys."

I wasn't in the mood to calm him down but I knew this would only escalate if I didn't make an attempt.

"Look, I did what I was paid to do. They gotta be happy with this deal. As long as Hugh pays him on time, it'll be okay. I gotta tell ya though, I'm not that happy with putting my dick on the line for either one of those two. I felt bad for her so I did it but I was never a fan of his."

Reilly had his eyes closed. "Yep, Sir Galahad to the rescue of the damsel once again."

I pulled over into a McDonald's, pissed. "What's your problem? You hooked me up with these assholes again and now it seems you can't distance yourself quick enough or far enough away. Did something happen after I left the Owl?"

He wouldn't look at me. Finally, he said, "He still owes me what he owes me. Made some lame excuse about cash flow. Same one he told you to use with Jabba the drug dealer. I'm back having to trust the guy and I completely do not trust the guy. And now you're involved."

I stared out the front window. I wasn't used to his feeling remorse.

"Look, I'm fine. He paid me. Once he trues it up with them, we're out of it. We'll get him to pay you out of the next deal. We'll find a way. You have my word on that. Okay?"

He nodded but I could tell he was skeptical. I wanted to cheer him up. "Jameson shots at the Owl? I'm buyin'."

He smiled a tight smile. "Damn straight, you're buyin'."

I sensed he was just going along with this but that he wasn't really convinced. I was sure that shots of Irish whiskey would help.

THIRTY-SEVEN

We found a parking space almost in front, unheard of these days. Reilly took his time getting out.

"What are ya, in a food coma?"

He looked at me strangely. "Nah, just not feeling that great." I let it slide but thought to myself that I needed to watch him.

The Owl, as usual, was jumping. On Wednesday's, they had local jazz musicians show up to jam. It could run the gamut from big band to be-bop to that avant-garde stuff, which reminded me of "Amadeus;" too many notes. Fortunately, tonight was leaning towards be-bop so the mood there was hectic and lively.

We found a table just as a couple of guys were getting up to leave. Callie came over almost immediately and took our drink orders. Gluten-free beer and a shot for Reilly, a shot for me with club soda back.

We listened for a while before either of us said anything. I was surprised he was tolerating this. Jazz was not usually on his dance card.

He finally spoke. "God, this shit is awful. Why does Glen allow this in here?"

Glen owned the Owl. He was there sporadically but I knew he was a jazz and blues fan. This was his idea. I looked around.

"Pretty good crowd for a Wednesday, though. Maybe there are more jazz buffs that you know in your philosophy, Horatio?"

I knew as soon as I said it that it was a mistake.

"What the fuck are you talking about? Who's Horatio?"

I waved it off. It was loud in there, too loud to explain Shakespeare. I caught Callie's eye for two more shots and as I did, a guy who had been sitting at the bar came over to our table.

"Can I join you?"

He was wearing a suit but no tie and looked like he sold insurance or real estate or timeshares. I shook my head.

"Sorry, pal. Private party. Not in the mood to entertain tonight."

He smiled a tight smile. "Mr. Shore, I think it would be to your benefit to speak with me."

I looked at him closely. It was dark in there but I was pretty sure I didn't know him. Reilly was looking now too, shifting his gaze from the guy to me and back.

"T, you know this guy?"

I shook my head. "I don't, but evidently he knows me. How do we know each other?"

He maintained that same tight smile. "Well, you don't know me but I know you. I know you both. Can we talk? Just you?" He flashed an FBI badge.

I looked at Reilly, who shrugged.

I turned back to the suit. "Not here, too noisy. There's a Starbucks on Chapel, next block up. Let's go there."

The suit stepped back and made a gesture of "You first". I got up, caught Callie's eye, told her I'd be back and looked at Reilly.

"I'm not back in a half hour, call in an Amber alert."

He saluted me as the suit and I walked out of the Owl.

It was warm out, a beautiful early June night in New Haven. There were people in the seats outside, including the street seats. A few years back, the city came to all of the restaurant and bar owners and offered to rent them a parking space in front of their establishments that they could cordon off and get extra seating out of. It pissed off people that were already finding it hard to find parking on the street, but the owners loved it and the city loved that it drove people into the city garages where they had to pay a lot more for parking. Everybody wins except the consumer.

We turned left at the corner and starting walking up Chapel. Roger, the homeless street guy, passed us and mumbled something about the FBI and the Apocalypse. Some said he was a clairvoyant. I was hoping they were wrong.

THIRTY-EIGHT

It was a usual weekday night at Starbucks. Every table was occupied by Yale students, most alone, staring deep into the morass of their laptops. I always thought that a bomb could go off and that they would only look up for a second and then Google the word "bomb".

We found a table in the back, near the rear emergency exit the management always kept locked.

Mr. No Name sat first, facing out so he could watch the room. I took my time sitting, looking around to see if there were others like him, forgetting that I suggested the place. On edge. Paranoid.

"So, is there a name or a number? 005 and a quarter?"

He looked at me and kept that tight smile going. Probably got an A in Stoic 101 at the Academy.

"Dillard, Mr. Shore, you can refer to me as Dillard. FBI Intelligence branch." He showed me the badge again.

I knew he had spoken this line this way many times

before, with different people, but I wasn't going to give him its desired effect.

"Only one name? Like Cher or Elton or Manson?"

The smile didn't change. "Ah yes, the famous Thomas Shore wit."

I affected my own mysterious smile. "Well, half the time at least." I was getting antsy.

"Look, I need to get back to the Owl. Reilly needs constant monitoring. What can I do for you, Mr. Dillard?"

He barely moved. "Just Dillard."

I was getting angry. "Okay. What can I do for you, Just Dillard?"

He took out an envelope from his side jacket pocket. Inside were a dozen or so photos. A couple of me, a few of Reilly, and the rest a variety of shots of members of the Druids. Each one was wearing their colors. I didn't recognize any of them and told Dillard as much.

"Nobody I know in that pile. Got any of your most recent vacation?"

He looked at me for a good 30 seconds. "Mr. Shore, this is not a joke. I'm not sure you're aware of how dangerous these people are. We know they're involved in many illegal practices, including murder and extortion. And, as you know, arson for hire. These are not people to mess around with. I seriously doubt they would find you as clever as you seem to find yourself."

I was done. "Look, Dillard, get to the point. If you're not going to tell me what you want, and we're not getting coffee, I'm going back to the Owl."

He seemed frustrated. I can have that effect on people.

"I know that two agents from the DEA have already spoken to you. I'm surprised you haven't heard from local law enforcement. We're all trying to do the same thing here, put an end to these people. We, the FBI, are asking you to help us. Information is the most valuable commodity there is in cases like this. Something you might tell us could be useful."

I looked around, then leaned forward until he did the same, lowering my voice to a whisper.

"You're gonna get me killed. I'll tell you what I told the Bobbsey twins, although I'm betting you know all this already. I had a case. There were bad guys that did business with the Druids. The bad guys are gone. The Druids are pissed. It cost them money. They'll either get over it or they won't. My guess is they're busy finding a new source of revenue or they're dealing with the local cops."

Dillard sat back and continued to watch me without saying a word. I got up and pushed in my chair for effect.

"Dillard, a pleasure. I'm out of here."

He reached into his other jacket pocket and pulled out a gold card case. I thought I saw a monogram. He flipped it open, pulled out a card and offered it to me. I took it. Nice stock.

"Mr. Shore, please make me the first call if anything comes to mind. The FBI is here to protect and serve. I think you can help us and we can certainly help you." Same tight smile.

I nodded but refrained from getting in the last word. I hit the door at a trot.

THIRTY-NINE

I ran/walked back to the Owl, not even stopping to browse my favorite window, CandiTopia, the confectionary store that sold all the great candy I grew up with. I needed to get back to check on Reilly.

He was where I left him but he had lain his head on the table. I wasn't sure if he was drunk or sleeping.

I shook him gently. "Hey."

He stirred and looked at me. I could tell he was in pain. "Exhausted, man. Need to sleep."

I motioned to Callie, got the check, paid it, and helped him up and out to the car. He was dead weight. I drove down to his place and found his space in back. After much maneuvering, I was able to get him into the apartment and resting on his couch. He fell asleep immediately.

I was exhausted myself. I went to his fridge to find a beer. I located a lone Guinness, found a glass, opened it and poured it out. The coldness of it combined with the dark, sweet flavor helped. I sat in his easy chair and passed out.

When I awoke an hour later, my brain was foggy and thought I heard voices downstairs. I reached in my pocket for my sap and tried to walk down the carpeted stairs without making a noise. I recognized Seamus's sister's voice as I got closer. She and Seamus were whispering. I hadn't heard her come in and I didn't hear him get up.

I startled them when I came around the corner from the stairwell. Kathy spoke first.

"Oh, hi, you're up. How do you feel?"

I shook my head. "I'm fine, how's he?" I pointed at Reilly, who seemed more alert but was still not himself.

Kathy looked at Seamus and then at me and then back to Seamus. Reilly was holding his head but spoke up

"I need to get out of myself. Tell us about the guy in the suit. I filled Kathy in on the rest of the day already."

I wasn't sure I wanted this many people involved but I knew Reilly trusted his sister implicitly.

"He was FBI. They want info on the Druids who have evidently been making threats towards me to each other. I know that not from the suit - whose name is Dillard - but from two DEA agents that got in my face the other night when I left the Owl after meeting with Hugh and Heather. They've been monitoring the Druids' phone calls so they heard the threats. They're pissed I messed up the deal they had with Callen."

Reilly was still holding his head but now he was shaking it as well. Kathy looked like the proverbial deer in a headlight. He spoke first.

"The FBI? The frickin' FBI? And the DEA? What the hell is this, a Robert Ludlum novel?"

I couldn't resist. "Ludlum wrote spy novels. This is more like James Patterson or Lee Child."

Reilly stared at me, incredulous. "You think this is funny? You think this is a joke?"

"I get that a lot these days." I was starting to get angry about the whole thing. "Look, I get that you've been dragged into this by default, but I'll fix it. If you want out, tell me now and you're out. I think these guys, the DEA and the FBI, are making too big of a deal out of this. I think it'll blow over before we know it and we'll all go back to being bored."

Kathy had been taking it all in but now spoke to Seamus directly. "Tell him."

Seamus leaned his head back and closed his eyes.

"Tell me what?" The source of their whispered conversation I interrupted.

Seamus was being cagey. "There's really nothing to tell. I've had some tests recently. The doctors are trying to be optimistic but they can't identify the problem. They think it could be pretty serious."

I sat there stunned. He hadn't let on about it. He looked terrible more often but I just chalked it up to the booze and the weed and working long, hard hours. That he could be sick never crossed my mind.

Kathy spoke up. "He's been taking meds for a little while now. It makes him drowsy. He's not supposed to be mixing it with alcohol but you know how he is. You can't really tell him anything."

I nodded. I didn't know what else to do. I decided to take charge and make a plan.

"Okay, look, I'm gonna crash here tonight and head home in the morning. We can figure this out tomorrow afternoon. I'll do whatever's necessary. I'll call the DEA guys or the FBI guy and try to put an end to all this, see if I can give them something that'll help them. We got nothing going on for a while, now that the Hugh thing is done. You can take it easier. The people that work for you can handle that stuff and I can be there when you have to get the tests done. Comprende?"

Reilly finally smiled. "God, I love it when you talk Spanish, Morticia."

I sneered. "It's French. I love it when you speak French, Morticia."

Reilly got up quickly. "All the same to me. French. Spanish. Pig Latin. I'm going to bed." And walked through a door into his bedroom.

Kathy and I looked at each other. "Guess he told us."

She laughed. "Guess he did." She yawned. "I'm going to bed too. See you tomorrow?"

I nodded. I was suddenly very tired.

FORTY

I woke up at 9 the next morning. I had been overtired, so it was a restless sleep on Reilly's couch. They were both still asleep so I washed up, made an espresso, drank it quickly, and left to walk back to my place. I stopped at the other Starbuck's on Church Street and grabbed a large Americano. There were a dozen people in there, even at this hour. It's true, America runs on coffee.

I walked the remaining two blocks to my apartment. There weren't many cars parked on the street so I couldn't help but notice the three motorcycles parked further down the block, in front of a restaurant that had been closed for a while. I couldn't imagine where the riders might be. There was no place to get breakfast on the street, except for Claire's, which was a vegetarian place. Didn't fit the stereotype of a biker but hey, who knows these days?

I shook it off as paranoia, right up until I walked into the lobby and the saw the three bikers sitting on the couch and chairs there.

Sam, the building's elderly doorman, was sitting behind his desk. He stood up quickly as soon as he saw me.

"Hey, Tommy, these fellas say they know you. I said they could wait here for you. Is that okay? I can call someone if need be?"

He glared at the one on the chair closest to him. It tipped me that he was probably the head guy.

"No worries, Sam. These fellas are here to see me. Business stuff."

I had been standing just inside the doorway. A young couple that had recently moved in came off the elevator and started walking towards the exit. They stopped short when they saw the five of us. I moved towards the door.

"Good morning, folks. Just about to leave. Come on through." I held the door open and they left. He gave me a weird look but she smiled at me. Nice couple.

I turned back to the boys but spoke to the head guy. "How about we go somewhere and talk?"

He got up, walked over to me and got close to my face. I could smell booze. He had blue eyes and affected a small soul patch. Like right out of biker central casting. "How about we go to your apartment and talk?"

I stepped back. "Ya know, good dental care is an important part of overall health. Just sayin'."

I looked into his eyes and kept my focus there. Show no fear.

He backed down a little. "Okay, we'll go across the street and get a coffee at the Owl and talk."

The other two got up. I walked out the door and the four of us crossed the street.

The Owl opened at 10 and Bill was working the

early shift. He had just unlocked the doors and looked up when we walked in, surprised to see customers so early.

"The coffee machine is warming up so it's gonna be a while, if you want coffee."

I put his mind at ease. "No worries, Bill. Just gonna go in the back and talk. Let us know when you're ready."

He grunted. I led the parade back to a grouping of easy chairs in the back of the bar, sitting with my back to the wall and with a view of the rest of the joint. Leader guy spoke first.

"You know who we are, right?"

I nodded I did but kept quiet.

"And you know what we want?"

I had a hunch but I wanted him to do all the talking. "No, you stumped me on that one."

He gave a look like he was talking to someone who wasn't all there.

"You cost us money. You need to make it right. We figure it at around fifteen thousand."

I laughed. "Dollars?"

Lead guy sat back in the chair. "We don't take credit cards."

My first thought was to tell him I did the wise-cracking around here. I thought better of it. Just as I was about to respond, Bill came over.

"Machine's up. You gentlemen want coffee?" He put a nasty inflection on "gentlemen".

I spoke first. "Love one, Bill. How about you boys?"

All three got up. They'd made their point. Lead guy hadn't stopped looking at me, even when Bill came over. "You got a week. Understand?"

I nodded and they left.

Bill watched them walk the length of the bar and go out, then turned back to me.

"What the hell was that about?"

I smiled at him. "Nothin'. Trying to sell me Girl Scout cookies. I told 'em I was dieting."

He scoffed. "You still want the coffee?"

I shook my head no. "I'll take a shot of Jameson, though."

I needed something to steady my hands.

FORTY-ONE

I got up and walked to the bar as Bill set up and poured the shot. I downed it quickly, threw a ten on the bar and walked outside. Looking right, I could see the three Druids still down the street, sitting on their bikes. One waved at me as I stood in front of the bar. They all started up with a loud roar and took off down College towards the highway.

I was about to cross the street to my apartment when the DEA unmarked pulled up. This time Macklin was driving and the Armani guy was in the passenger seat. He rolled down the window but Macklin leaned over and asked me, "Everything good?"

I squatted down to window level. "Just a visit from the Druids...but I'm betting you already knew that."

Macklin smiled. "We were watching from up the street. We figured you could hold your own. Did you find out who they were, get names? What did they want?"

I hadn't figured out how I was going to handle this yet so I decided to keep my cards close to the vest.

"They're having a fundraiser. Want me to perform magic."

Macklin sat back in the seat and looked straight ahead.

"Okay, wiseguy. Suit yourself."

Then floored it, cutting off another car and nearly knocking me over. I righted myself, shaking my head, then walked across to my apartment.

Sam came up to me as I went in, clearly shaken. "Sorry, Tommy, they were here a while. I thought about calling the cops but I wasn't sure if they were really friends of yours or what. I'm really sorry."

I tried to calm him down. "Not your fault, Sam. You did fine."

I left him and went to my apartment. Once I got inside, I found Dillard's card and called him. He answered on the second ring.

"Mr. Shore. What can I do for you?"

Man, I hate Caller ID. "I just got a visit from three of the Druids. I'm calling you, even though the DEA guys asked me out first."

I heard him sigh. I got that a lot. "What did they want? Did you get names?"

Jeez, they're all the same. "No names. They want money. They think I owe them for taking Callen out, that I cost them revenue. They want 15K."

I heard a soft whistle and then a long pause. I wondered if he was still on the line. "Dillard?"

"Yeah, still here. Just looking at their files. Was the one who did all the talking short, blues eyes, silly little jazz beard?"

"That's a soul patch, Dillard. Get the vernacular

right if you're gonna hang with these boys. Yeah, that's the one. Who is he?"

"James Barton. He's the Sergeant-at-Arms. He's in charge of discipline and weapons. I'm betting the other two were prospects."

Now it was my turn to sigh. Discipline and weapons.

He went on. "I told you, these are dangerous men that you can't screw around with. You're gonna get badly hurt or killed. Let us help you."

I decided to hear him out. "Okay, what would I need to do?"

He paused, then answered. "Wear a wire. Set up another meet and get it on tape."

Nope. "Look, I didn't set this first meet up, they were waiting for me in the lobby of my apartment. It was meant to scare me. It did what it was intended to do. But I can't wear a wire. That's crazy, they'd definitely kill me if they caught me bugged."

He continued to try and convince me, telling me that it wasn't like TV or the movies, that they have undetectable devices now. I wasn't buying any of it.

"I gotta think. They gave me a week. I'll call you in a few days."

I hung up and thought that this day couldn't get any worse. And, just like in the movies and on TV, the phone rang. And it got worse.

FORTY-TWO

It was Hugh. I had called and left a message with Heather to call me but Hugh called instead. I wanted to tell her what had gone down and the arrangement I made. Now I would need to deal with him.

After some forced pleasantries, I gave him the details of the deal I had made. There was silence, until he cleared his throat.

"A week, huh? I'm not sure I can do a week. I thought I asked you to ask for two or three?"

I felt my skin get hot. I tried to control my anger.

"Well, I didn't have a whole lot of choice here. He thought he was being magnanimous by giving you a week. Besides, that's the time frame we spoke about when we met at the Owl. You said you had some deals pending and needed a week."

He wasn't responding. I knew from past experience with him that he was trying to figure an angle.

"Look, I can't stress this enough. You need to make this happen. If you don't, he will come see you. And my gut feeling is, that won't be a good thing. For anyone.

Including me. He threatened me, too. And I don't really respond well to threats."

There was silence again. Finally, he said, "Okay, I have something going this Saturday. I should have enough cash to pay him and extra to buy more weed. Monday or Tuesday. Will that work?"

I told him it would and hung up. I immediately called Reilly. No answer. I left a message.

I was livid. This guy would hang us out to dry as sure as look at us. I felt bad for Heather but he was quickly making that feeling go away. I worked the heavy bag I had hung up in the back room until I felt the anger dissipate. And then Reilly called me back and it flooded back. I picked up after one ring.

"I spoke to that asshole Hugh. He doesn't have the cash. He needs more time, says he told me to ask for two weeks. I could kill him."

I heard coughing. "Yeah, hello to you, too. What the fuck?"

I tried to relax myself and breathe. "Hey. Sorry, but I knew this guy was bad news and so far, I'm not wrong. Only now, I'm tied into his paying his debt. And the last thing I need is a 400-pound drug dealer and his posse looking for me. I already have a biker gang that aren't happy with me. Throw in my ex-wife and it'll be the holy trinity of misery."

I was aware I was ranting. Reilly was surprisingly calm.

"Look, he'll get the money together. He will. He says he's different now and I believe him."

Once again, shock. "Why? Why do you believe him? You told me the other day you didn't trust him. Why the change of heart?"

Reilly was quiet. When he spoke, it was in a controlled voice, as if he was trying to maintain his composure.

"T, I have to start having a large barrage of tests. They're expensive, and not fully covered by my insurance. I start in two weeks. It's imperative that I get that cash from Hugh before then. I have to believe that he's going to get it to me. I'm out of options."

Now it was my turn to be silent, lost in thought. This had gotten complicated quickly and was now a matter of life and death. After 30 seconds or so, I could hear Reilly breathing hard and it snapped me back to earth.

"Alright, okay...we can figure this out. I need to think. Give me a few days to come up with a plan. We can figure something out. "

I was nervous, talking fast. I took a breath.

"Let's meet Friday at the Owl for drinks, the usual time, 7:30 or so, yeah? Does that sound right?"

He agreed but I could tell his heart wasn't in it. It didn't matter. I needed him to know I would help him.

I set about to planning how I was going to do just that.

FORTY-THREE

I spent the next two days trying to come up with a plan
but it was difficult. Every idea I came up with involved
too many contingencies. Would Hugh get the cash? Iffy
at best. Would the DEA or the FBI be willing to go
along with it? I'm not sure I could involve them and
come out unscathed. Could I pull it off by myself?
Reilly was out of the picture and there were few others
I could trust to walk the fine line between legal and
illegal.

I was laying low. I had a few good takeout meals
delivered to the apartment and tried to stay away from
the Owl and my other usual haunts.

On Thursday night, I decided I needed to get out of
my head for a while. I glanced at the fridge door and
saw the invitation to the birthday party. I would call
Rosalind.

I'd met her at the Owl a few months back. She was
a nurse at Yale New Haven hospital and once a week
she and her co-workers would go out somewhere for
drinks. The night we met, they had been to dinner at

Barcelona, a decent Spanish restaurant on Temple Street. Afterwards, they'd walked up the alley to the Owl. She was sitting at the bar and was almost ready to leave when Reilly went off on a rant. It had amused her and her laugh had intrigued me. We started talking and I asked her if she would have dinner with me. We went to Union League, the same place that her kids would be holding her birthday party. I wondered if our going there prompted that and planned to ask her.

I found her number on the same slip of paper she had originally written it on, tacked up by a magnet right next to the invite. She answered on the third ring.

"Well, as I live and breathe, Tommy Shore!" She had a wicked sense of humor and loved to tease. I enjoyed it.

"The one and only. Thought I had left these parts to explore the West Indies, eh?"

She laughed. "Nothing so romantic. Maybe gone underground because of threats from some irate husband or father!"

I smiled. I loved her playfulness. "Nothing so romantic. How have you been?

I could hear her sit down, settling in.

"I've been well. Busy at work. Not a lot new but every day brings something to make me happy." She paused. "Did you get the invitation?"

I had been holding back, unsure if it was a surprise that I didn't want to spoil. "I did."

She laughed again. "And? Playing hard to get? Are you going to come?"

I hadn't decided yet. Meeting her family was a big step and I wasn't sure we were there yet. We had been on one more date in the past two months. Another terrific dinner at Caseus and no interruptions from fires and the like. We been trying to find time for a third but it had been difficult, mostly because of her schedule and rotating shifts. This would ratchet things up a bit.

"Do you want me to come? Not just let it be your family?"

Another pause. "I asked them to invite you. I had a wonderful time on the two dates we've been on and I couldn't think of anyone I wanted to be there more than you."

I felt myself blushing and couldn't remember the last time that happened. I told her as much. "I'm blushing like a schoolgirl." She laughed again.

We talked easily, with her filling me in on the things that were happening at work and with her family and me skirting around the new case and the predicament I found myself in.

After an hour, she said she needed to go to sleep but that she was happy I'd called. I waited a few seconds to let that sink in. "Talking to you makes me happy as well. I'd love to come to your party. I'll RSVP in the morning."

I could tell that made her happy. We said goodnight and hung up.

It was the first night I slept soundly without booze in a while.

FORTY-FOUR

I woke up early on Friday and decided I would get out and treat myself to breakfast. I showered, dressed, and walked up Chapel Street to Heirloom in the Study Hotel. I had stayed away from the place when it first opened, based on the pretentiousness of its name, but a friend took me there for breakfast and I was converted. I'd been there for drinks at night and it had its share of hipsters and wannabes, but the breakfast they served was great and reasonable.

After I'd eaten, I decided to take a walk. I went to the corner and turned up Park Street. It was lined with old houses, only changing near the top of the street. Tarry Lodge was there, a terrific Neo-Italian place, part of a chain but excellent. I shook my head at the travails of Mario Batali and thought it must have been the shoes. But the chopped salumi salad and the calzones there were amazing and I made a mental note to take Rosalind there one of these days.

I crossed the street at the parking lot on Broadway and went into the Yale Co-op to browse. It had become a Barnes and Noble in the past few years but I remembered when it was privately owned and overstuffed with books, Yale merchandise, records, CDs, junk food and clothing. It was neat and tidy now but some of the charm had also disappeared.

I walked down Broadway, shaking my head again at the Apple store that was packed this early in the morning, and looking at the gentrification that seemed to have affected this street more than most. Urban Outfitters, Patagonia, J Crew - all the names were here for students to spend their stipends in. I missed the old stores like Cutler's Records and Whitlock's Rare Books. Even the food joints got fufu. The Educated Burger was replaced by Salsa Fresca and the Yankee Doodle crowd was now being serviced by Maison Mathis. It made me sad.

I turned up York Street and stopped in at Blue State Coffee. Started in Providence, they had grown quickly and had two locations in New Haven. They liked to bill themselves as a community-oriented shop but I liked their house blend much more than the community they attracted. I don't own a fedora and would be hard-pressed to get my hair to stay up in a bun. Still, it was tasty Joe.

I took my coffee in a to-go cup and kept walking up York until I came to Grove, then crossed the street and went into the Grove Street cemetery.

The Grove Street Cemetery was the first chartered burial ground in the U.S. After an epidemic of Yellow Fever in the late 1700s, the city stopped burying folks on the green and started burying them here. It was a who's who of historical names, from Eli Whitney to

Glen Miller, from Roger Sherman to Noah Webster and Walter Camp.

I liked it here. You entered on through a beautiful gateway, done in the Egyptian Revival Style. The inscription, "The Dead Shall Be Raised" greets you. It was a great place to spend a few hours to think.

I strolled the grounds for quite a while, reading the names and looking at the ornate graves. When I came upon a grave stone for Theodore Winthrop, I stopped short. He had been a Major in the army during the Civil War and had been the first New Havener to die in that war. I had always been fascinated about that period of our history and read extensively on it. I had a large collection of books, including first editions by Shelby Foote and Ambrose Bierce. One of my favorites was *The Killer Angels* by Michael Shaara, a historical novel that centered on four days at Gettysburg.

I was thinking about Gettysburg when the idea hit. I left the cemetery in a hurry and ran down College to my apartment.

I had a plan.

FORTY-FIVE

When I got back to the apartment, there were two messages waiting, one from Hugh and one from Heather. I picked hers up first.

"Tommy, this is Heather. I really need to talk to you. It's really important. Please call me as soon as you get in. It's about Hugh and the money."

Now I was curious about Hugh's message. I hit the button to play the next one.

"Tom, this is Hugh. Look, I'm not completely sure I can get the cash we need for Monday. I'll know more tomorrow. Is there any way, any way at all that you can get me more time? Call me back." And left me a phone number.

I stared at the machine. He sounded like he had been drinking. The plan I was considering was contingent on his having the cash needed to pay back White Clarence so taking that out of play would cause major issues.

I called Heather. She picked up immediately. I

could tell she had been crying. "Hey there. It's Tommy. What's up?"

She started sobbing again. I waited until she collected herself. After a minute, she seemed to have it under control.

I kept my voice soft to keep her calm. "Tell me what's up, Heather."

I could hear her getting her breath. "Tommy, Hugh's being an asshole. He's been drinking all day and says he doesn't have the cash you need. Says he's gonna bet it all on the Belmont tomorrow to get what we need. Says he has a sure thing. He's got about five grand I know about. I asked him to give that to you, maybe you could make that work and get us another week, but I don't think he actually has another plan. I think betting on the race was his plan all along."

She was crying again. I silently cursed Reilly for getting me involved with these people.

"Heather, calm down. Hugh called me and left a message. I need to call him back. After I talk to him, I'll call you back and we'll go from there. Okay?"

She agreed and we hung up. I dialed the number Hugh left on my machine. There was no answer. I tried it two more times but it kept ringing. I hung up after the third time. My phone rang immediately. It was Hugh.

"Hi, Tom. I was screening calls. Had to be sure it was you."

I wasn't in the mood for this but I couldn't resist. "You don't have caller ID?"

He paused. "I had to be sure they didn't have you and were making you call me."

What an asshole. "How do you know they don't now? Because I tried three times? Are you that stupid?"

Another pause. Guess he decided to ignore that. "Did you get my message?"

"I called you on the number you left me, moron. Of course, I got the message." This was going nowhere quickly. "Look, I spoke to Heather. She told me your plan. It's not going to work. You can't..."

He interrupted to say how it was a sure thing, how he knew a guy who knew a guy who had a fix in. That he could bet "show" at 2 to 1 and double his money, giving us what we needed to pay back Clarence. I bristled at the "us" part.

"Hugh, let me have the five K. I can try and reason with him again. The cash in hand might convince him. There will be more vig to pay but it's our best shot."

The plan I was making went out the window.

"Tom...Tommy...this is a sure thing. I can make it work. Trust me. This guy owes me big time. It's good info. I'll have the ten Grand on Monday like I promised. And I'll talk to Heather." I tried to argue some more but he had already hung up.

I sat down at the kitchen table and looked around the place. I would have to put my plan on hold. I would have to wait until Monday and see what that day brings.

FORTY-SIX

Later that night, I went to the Owl. Friday nights could go either way there, weird or normal. Sometimes it was a class crowd. Early birds waiting to go to the Shubert theatre or the College Street Music Hall, having a drink and a smoke beforehand. The after- dinner crowd looking to unwind so they can digest expensive food with a cigar and a cognac.

But it could also be filled with frat boys trying to look cool with a cigar in one hand and a cheap beer in the other or first timers checking out the vibe and trying to get used to the smoke.

Our usual table was open so I sat down on a stool facing the door to wait for Reilly. I did a quick scan of the back of the place and down the bar to see if there was anyone that triggered any alarms. All good.

I ordered a club soda. Drinking would come later. I lit up a Padron 1926. Felt like treating myself.

Reilly walked in around 8:30 and sat down. He leaned forward to conspire. "So, where are we?"

I looked at him. "Where are WE? We're nowhere.

Your buddy Hugh screwed the pooch. He doesn't have the cash we need to make the deal but thinks he's got a sure thing at tomorrow's Belmont, that he can hit a 2 to 1 shot and get the ten grand I made the deal with. He's an idiot. I can't believe I let you get me involved with this guy."

I let that sink in as Reilly tried to wrap his head around it. He finally looked up and asked, "Did he mention the name of the horse?"

I let out a sharp laugh. "Are you kidding me? THAT'S your response? To bet the horse yourself? Are you an idiot, too? When has one of Hugh's schemes ever paid off, for anyone? He still owes you what, five grand?"

Reilly lowered his eyes. "Eight."

I laughed again. "Eight? Eight. He owes you eight grand? And you're willing to trust this guy? Maybe you're a moron, too."

I was livid, mostly at myself. I let him get me into something I knew was wrong, chasing quick cash. Now I was waiting to hear whether my life would be turned upside down on a horse race.

Reilly looked hard at me and said, "Let's do shots. Nothin' we can do about any of it now, eh?"

Seamus Reilly, Zen master. I gave up, nodded and he went to the bar to order a round.

As he was ordering, I noticed two guys come in that looked vaguely familiar. As I stared, I realized that they were two of White Clarence's posse that he made sit at the second table. Coincidence or sent here to keep an eye on me?

They took the two first seats at the bar, the only ones that had recently opened. I could see them order then glance my way. I know that they saw me but weren't acknowledging I was there. So I walked over and stood behind them.

"Hey there, boys, welcome to the Owl. Come here a lot?"

The one on my left looked over his shoulder and pretended not to recognize me. "Do we know you?"

I laughed. "Not personally but we did have dinner together. Well, I should say, you had dinner. I spent most of the time keeping my limbs out of the way of the food. Y'all are one hungry bunch. Growing boys and all."

They looked at each other and the one on my right shrugged. Tweedle Dee on the left spoke up.

"Okay, we're supposed to eyeball you and tell you that you only have until Tuesday to get WC his money."

I know he meant it to seem like a natural threat but it came out like he'd been practicing it in a mirror.

I laughed again.

"You can tell WC that he doesn't have to worry, that he'll get his money, plus a significant order for new product. Tell him he needs to be ready and that I'll reach out with details on Monday. Can you both remember all that?"

They both looked at each other, nodded their heads, finished their drinks and left.

I went back to the table. Reilly had downed his shot and mine. I looked at him, shook my head, and went to the bar to buy another round.

FORTY-SEVEN

I stayed in bed until late on Saturday morning, nursing a hangover. We had stayed at the Owl until 1:00 and had done rounds of shots every hour until. After a while, strangers were buying them for us and we became the center of everyone's good time. I knew I would pay for it today but I didn't care at the time.

I showered, dressed, made coffee and then sat down to put down on paper the plan I had been thinking about since I saw Theodore Winthrop's grave in the Grove Street cemetery.

Major Teddy Winthrop was from New Haven. He was arguably one of the first casualties of the Civil War and may or may not have been the first officer killed in that war.

He met his demise at the Battle of Big Bethel. I'd always loved the name of that one. There was evidently a little Bethel but this battle had been fought on the larger plane.

The Confederate Army was slick there. They'd sent a few small troops to set up camp, to lure the

Union army in. When the info came back to the Union guys that there was a small band of soldiers, they took the bait. When they attacked, the Union soldiers ended up firing upon themselves until the Rebels swooped in. Most of the Union army got wiped out.

Major Winthrop led the charge, his superior officer deciding he would wait behind. Management.

As the battle heated up, Winthrop supposedly yelled, "One more charge boys, and the day is ours," and then caught a musket ball in the head.

I had forgotten the story but walking by the grave reminded me of it and gave me an idea to use with White Clarence and the Druids: pit themselves against each other and duck. The last thing I wanted was a musket ball to the head.

I wrote it all down on a yellow legal pad, then read it over.

My first thought was that White Clarence and the Druids would be a great name for a band.

My second thought was that this was all dependent on how Hugh did today or the entire plan would go up in smoke.

My third thought was the usual one: I'm hungry.

I walked out the side door of my building and went down to Temple Street. A new Laotian restaurant had opened on the street and the word was they had the best pho in town. It was in their name: Pho Ketkeo, named after the owner and what they did best. A good sign.

I stopped in, sat down at the counter and ordered a large bowl. When it came, it was delicious: sweet broth, noodles, beef, herbs and spices. Even in the summer, it revitalizes the body.

Afterwards, I walked down Temple and went in to the Criterion theatre. I usually had nothing in mind that I wanted to see, but instead would just pick something that looked good and go in. It had worked for me in the past.

I settled on a movie about a woman running a high stakes poker game, directed by the guy who wrote the West Wing. It was based on a true story. I liked it well enough and it killed a few hours.

I headed back up Crown and up College. I would sit in the Owl, have a smoke and a coffee and watch the Belmont. I still didn't know the name of Hugh's horse so it would be a horse race for me. Too much inside info tended to spoil the event.

I used to love the Triple Crown. Every year, my ex-wife and I and a bunch of friends would go to Sports Haven, to watch and bet all three. The Derby was the big one, with the hats and dresses. The Preakness was my favorite, as I loved being in Maryland the few times I had gone down there. The Belmont always felt like an afterthought but we all cheered whenever there was a chance at a Triple Crown winner. Got close a few times but nothing until a few years ago when American Pharaoh finally did it. It was great to watch but it had taken the bloom off the racing rose for me.

I got my usual seat, with a perfect view of the TV and ordered an Americano from Callie. I liked the summer. There were still students around from the summer school but you could always find seats in restaurants and there was plenty of parking. It got busier as it got closer to post time and when the race went off, it was crowded.

It was a good race, close. The longest of the three at

a mile and a half, the field usually only has 10-12 horses instead of the 20 the Derby has. Today had nine and it was neck and neck until the stretch when a horse named Always Dreaming came from behind and almost won it. I found myself hoping that was Hugh's horse.

I finished my Americano, gave Callie a ten, and left.

In my apartment, I poured myself a shot of Jameson and watched television until I fell asleep.

It was a good day. They were few and far between.

FORTY-EIGHT

The phone ringing woke me out of a deep sleep the next day. I had been dreaming about a horse that talked, who kept telling me that he was going to win the big race. As I came awake, I found myself hoping that that wasn't Hugh's insider.

I picked up the phone on the fifth ring. It was Hugh.

"Tom, Hugh. You weren't sleeping, were you? Shank of the day, man, shank of the day. Rise and shine."

Way too hyper for this hour of the morning.

"What do you need, Hugh?"

He was taking his time, savoring this. "Well, great news, amigo, great news. My horse came in second. Always Dreaming. Perfectly named, no?"

The come from behind horse. "Yes, that is great news. So, you have the cash, all $10K? And you wanted to buy more. You'll have the cash for that? WC was expecting you to do more business."

I was trying to be careful. Dillard talking about phone taps made me wary.

"I have all we need. Bet him to place instead of to show. Won about $20K, ten for Clarence and five to buy more with. And five for me to play with."

I noticed how the "five to play with" excluded Heather. I wanted this over with.

"Can you get me the cash today? I'm going to need to set it up to pay him and make the exchange for more. He gave me until Tuesday and I definitely want to meet that deadline."

There was a pause. Never a good sign with Hugh.

"I can get you the money first thing tomorrow. I need to see my bookie first and collect."

I leaned back and stared at the ceiling. This couldn't end soon enough.

"You haven't got the money then?"

His voice took on a whiny quality. "Tommy, I'll get it. It's done, a sure thing. I asked for it in hundreds. Fifteen packs of ten one hundred-dollar bills, okay?"

I took my time answering, made him sweat a little.

"Okay. Meet me at Caseus at one. I'll be having lunch, the window seat to the far right as you come in the door. Just you. No Heather. I mean it this time, Hugh. I see Heather and the whole thing is off. I'll deal with my own consequences."

He agreed and hung up.

I went back to bed, thinking that, if I just shut my eyes and emptied my head of all thoughts, I could fall back asleep. No such luck.

The plan I was considering was dangerous, with a hundred ways it could go wrong. These were bad people that were used to doing bad things. There would be guns. I considered carrying a piece.

I didn't own one but I knew how to use one and was a good shot. I had a cop friend who loved them that used to take me out to a range in Hamden for target practice. We went a lot, once a week, and he would bring all kinds of caliber with us. I still remember the kick back from the .357. After firing that, I understood the damage it could do.

There was only one guy I knew who could get me a gun on such short notice. I called Mickey.

We had met at anger management community service. I knew right off he was connected and spent more time on the wrong side of the law than in the right. He would know how to connect me to a gun.

I was still suspicious from my conversation with Dillard so I rummaged through my desk and found an old burner phone and a charger cord. I plugged it in, waited a bit until I had some bars, then threw on some clothes and went outside near the dumpsters in the back alley. I got out the last number I had for him and dialed.

"Yeah?" Gruff and no-nonsense.

"Mickey, its Tommy Shore." He wasn't one for pleasantries.

"Tommy! I didn't recognize the number. You on a burner? Whattya need?"

Always straight to the point. "I need a piece, nothing fancy, something easy, just-in-case protection."

"Sure...38 work?" No questions.

"Yeah, that'd be great. Where and when? Owl?"

There was a pause. "Nah, too open. There's a diner

in Hamden, the Acropolis, on Dixwell. Let's have breakfast in the morning."

I agreed to meet him at 8:30 the next morning.

I would need a car for a few days. I went back into the apartment, called Hertz and arranged to pick one up. The branch near the train station was open until 2:00 so I changed my clothes and walked down there, stopping at Starbucks on the corner of Church for an Americano. Priorities.

The regular guy was off at the Hertz place so it took longer than usual. I got into a blue Camry and went to get on 95, towards West Haven. A little reconnaissance never hurt anyone.

FORTY-NINE

I got off the highway at the First Avenue exit, turned left and went down to Elm Street. I stayed on that street over Campbell Avenue and past the burger joints and the stores until I hit a bevy of old warehouses and factories.

I was looking for a place to meet with White Clarence and give him the money. It needed to be secluded but open at the same time.

I drove around for an hour. I was about to call it a day when I turned up a side street and found the perfect location.

About halfway down that street was an abandoned factory where, according to a faded sign, they used to make girdles. Behind the factory, on the other side of a fence, were railroad tracks. And between the tracks and the back of the factory was an access road that must have been where delivery trucks drove around to drop off materials. There were three boarded up docks, each with a platform and stairs leading up to an entry door. I looked around. You would need to be on the tracks to see anything that was happening on that road. Or in the factory.

I parked next to the first platform. The bay door had been heavily graffitied and the bottom left corner had been partially kicked in. The entry door to the left of the bay door was padlocked. I tried to see if there was any way to get in through the kicked in part but it was too small.

The second bay seemed intact as well and the door was also padlocked.

I drove down to the last bay and the first thing I saw was no padlock on the door. I muttered "Bingo, Goldilocks" to myself.

I got out, walked up the stairs and tried the door. It was latched from inside but I suspected a flimsy bolt lock that would give way to a well-placed boot heel.

I also noticed a window just past the door that was not completely boarded up. It was higher than I could reach so I drove the car down to it, got up on the hood, and stood so I could look inside. It was dark but I could see abandoned machinery and hundreds of wooden pallets in various stacks. A perfect place to meet and do the exchange. There wouldn't be much light but I could bring some flashlights and we could stay close to the windows. It might work.

I got back in the car and got back on the highway.

Instead of heading downtown, I stayed on 95 until I was halfway over the Pearl Harbor Memorial Bridge. Known to locals as the Q Bridge, it goes over the Quinnipiac River into East Haven. It had been renamed in 1995 to commemorate Pearl Harbor. The state then spent a half billion dollars to replace it with ten lanes of traffic. It was much prettier now but still jammed up at rush hour, especially on Fridays leading into a holiday weekend.

I got off the highway halfway across the bridge at an exit that brought you into the harbor area from the back.

New Haven Harbor had an interesting history. Protected by a peninsula on its east shore that holds a huge lighthouse, the British had once tried to land there during the Revolutionary War. They were met by Patriots who successfully defended it. East Haven residents point to it as a yet another reason not to mess with them.

I drove around the backstreets until I got to Forbes Avenue and pulled into the lot of the Realm Cafe. It was a bar that doubled as a strip club...inside a church.

It was also a known hangout of the Druids.

I went in the side entrance and waited a few minutes for my eyes to adjust. It was cool in there, with the air turned way up.

There were two horseshoe bars, with a runway running down the middle of both. A couple of girls going through the motions were dancing to music coming from two tinny speakers overhead. It sounded like Prince but I couldn't be sure.

On the far right was a room that was more brightly lit than the main room. I could hear the crack of pool balls. I headed there.

Inside were the two Druids that came to see me with Barton. They were playing. Two other Druids were sitting on stools on the side of the table. They all looked up when I entered.

"Gentlemen...how goes it? Is your fearless leader around?"

One of the guys with the pool cue in his hand

started laughing. He turned to the two on the stools and said, "This is the guy. This is the guy we were telling you about that took out Callen." The one on the stool closest to me sneered. "This guy?"

Lucky for me I have high self-esteem.

"I'm looking for Barton." I could see they were surprised that I knew his name. "Let him know I'll have the money Tuesday. Have him call me here." I gave them the burner number. Then turned and walked out.

It took everything I had not to stop at the bar for a shot of Jameson to steady my hands.

FIFTY

I drove back to my apartment as fast as possible, following Forbes Avenue and then over the backstreets. I parked in the garage next to the Taft and walked down the back staircase to keep from being seen from the street. I was able to go in the side door and into my apartment quickly.

I made a phone call to Dillard and left a message to call me. Hopefully, he would pick it up early Monday morning. I also called the DEA guy, Macklin. He actually picked up.

"Well, if it isn't Mike Hammer. What's shakin', sunshine?"

I lowered my voice like I was bringing him into my confidence. "Listen, I don't have anything on the bikers but I need your help. A good friend has gotten involved with some drug dealers from West Haven. A guy named White Clarence."

I could tell he was holding a hand over the speaker and relaying my words to his partner, who would probably run the info through the computer. He came back on almost immediately.

"What's going on?"

I needed to play to their wanting to make me indebted to them.

"A friend set up a meeting with him. There's going to be about 50 grand worth of weed changing hands. I don't trust this Clarence guy to hold up his end of the bargain. I wasn't sure how to approach this. I thought you fellas could help me."

I exaggerated the weight to make it enticing enough for them to care. I needed him to feel like he was doing me a favor, that I would owe him.

"I know its small potatoes for guys like you but you told me to call you first with anything I knew about. I'm trying to protect my friend and wasn't sure which way to go." Plaintive, almost whiny.

It was quiet for a solid minute. I could hear whispering. Finally, Macklin got back on.

"Shore, I think we can help you. The hard part will be keeping your friend from getting caught up in the middle of this. Where is this exchange taking place?"

"That's great, thank you. It's somewhere in West Haven. I'll know more tomorrow or Tuesday. It's supposed to go down on Tuesday."

Macklin said something to his partner again then addressed me, his voice harder this time.

"Shore, we help you with this thing, we're gonna need payback. It's gonna cost us a few favors. We're gonna need you to work with us on this Druids thing after it's over."

There it was. They had taken the bait. I answered in the most contrite voice I could conjure up.

"I totally understand. Thank you. Whatever it takes to make it right when it's over, you can count on me."

We hung up after I assured them that I would call as soon as I heard the details.

I wasn't off the phone a minute when it rang.

"Mr. Shore, Dillard. You called and left a message? What can I do for you?"

Time to put part two into place.

"Dillard, like I told you, the Druids want me to pay them for their lost income, $15K. I don't have the money but I know about an exchange that's going down where that kind of money will be in play. I'm trying to arrange for them to be there, assuming they would find a way to take that money for themselves. I was thinking you may want to be there as well?"

I heard Dillard chuckle. "Let me get this straight. There's a deal going down where money is being exchanged and you're trying to get the Druids to take it down to pay your debt to them? I underestimated you, Shore. That takes some brass to try and pull off. And now you want me to take them down while they're doing it?"

I was nodding the entire time as I heard him recite the plan back to me. "Yeah, that pretty much sums it up."

I could feel some hesitation on his part. He had more questions. FBI training.

"And where are you going to be while all this goes down?"

I thought I'd had him. "I'll be there. I need to get them to a place where they won't suspect, but also think they have surprise on their side. As soon as I know times and location, I can call you. I'll make sure you have enough time to get your guys in place."

He was still hesitant. "This feels like there's too many ways it can go wrong. I'm not sure I'm comfortable having you in the middle of it."

I needed to be firm. "I'm in the mix, end of story. They won't do this unless I'm there."

He still wouldn't commit. "I'm going to have to get back to you, check with my superiors."

Damn. "Okay, you do what you need to do. This thing goes down Tuesday. Call me and let me know your decision. I should know location and time by tomorrow, Tuesday morning latest."

I hung up. Dillard was iffy. Hugh was a question mark. The DEA boys were in. I still had to hear from the Druids and I still had to call White Clarence.

All this manipulation was making me hungry. I realized it had been a while. I called Reilly. He picked up on the 2nd ring. Shocking.

"Did you eat yet?" He hadn't.

"Meet me at Bar in 20 minutes?"

Bar was a pizza joint and a brewery. They made great pizza and put themselves on the New Haven Pizza map by offering weird toppings, including mashed potatoes. It sounded strange but it actually worked. Not all the time but every once in a while.

I walked down to Crown Street, cutting through the Yale parking lot. It was starting to fill up with tourists, Yalies and out-of-towners in to see a show at the Shubert.

I knew the owner and he took me past the line and over to a back booth. The waitress came over and I ordered a tasting flight of two of the beers they made,

Toasted Blonde and Damn Good Stout. She brought over 2 small glasses of each in a rack. I took a sip of the blonde ale just as Reilly came in.

He was out of breath but grabbed a glass of the stout and asked, "For me?" I nodded and he downed it.

I asked him why he was so winded. "I biked here. It's locked up outside. Didn't feel like trying to find parking."

I was impressed and told him so. He shrugged. We were both tired. I had ordered an Eggplant/Bacon pizza and it showed up 5 minutes after he sat down.

We ate in silence.

FIFTY-ONE

I got up early Monday and drove out to Hamden. The Acropolis diner had been there forever and served a decent breakfast. Mickey was in the back booth, waiting.

"Tommy, howyadoin'?" He was eating a couple of eggs and toast and had been reading the Post, the Daily News sitting on the table. He folded the paper in half and put it on top of the other paper, then pushed it towards me.

"Have you read what our cockamamie Prez did today?"

I picked up both papers without looking and placed them on the seat beside me, feeling the weight of the piece underneath.

I smiled at him. "Crazy times we're living in, eh?"

He smiled back. "Ya got that right." He held my gaze. "You sure about this?"

I nodded. "What do I owe you?"

He went back to his eggs. "We're good. Be careful, amigo."

I nodded again and left, paying his tab at the cash register on the way out.

I drove back to the apartment and found a space in front. I parked, brought the papers into the apartment, then went back out and walked around the block, stopping at the deli for a buttered hard roll and a coffee. I took them down to the green and found a bench and sat and ate the roll and sipped the coffee. I was killing time until I had to meet Hugh. It was warm and people were sitting on blankets reading and a few throwing a Frisbee around. I watched for a while.

Around 10:30, I got up and walked back to the apartment. I took a shower, made more coffee, and sat and read the two papers Mickey had passed the gun to me under. When I was done, I spread them out on the kitchen table and placed the gun on top. I had an old cleaning kit that I had gotten down from a cupboard and I opened it and starting cleaning it. When I was done, I emptied the small leather bag that had been with the gun and six bullets fell out. I loaded them into the gun and spun the cylinder. I was ready.

I went over to the Owl to meet Hugh. He was already there, sitting at the bar. Points for punctuality.

I walked over to him. He was drinking coffee, a good sign.

He smiled when he saw me.

"Thomas. Good to see you."

Thomas. I let it slide.

"Hugh. Thanks for being on time. Do you have the money?"

He laughed. "Always to the point, eh?" He reached down under the bar and took a bag off the hook there. I looked at it as he opened the ties and reached inside. It was purple and looked like velvet. Whatever else, the guy had his own style.

Inside that bag was a crumpled brown lunch bag, filled with fifteen bundles, each bundle holding 10 one hundred-dollar bills. So much for style.

He looked at me and got serious.

"So, what's the plan?"

I needed to be careful here. Too much information can be a bad thing.

"I'm going to meet with Clarence, give him the 10 grand you owe him, get 4 Grand of product, call you and deliver the product."

His head jerked up. "You mean five Grand of product, right?"

I looked at him and waited. He would get it soon enough. It only took 30 seconds.

"And you're taking a thousand for yourself. I see. Thought I had already paid you."

I kept my smile tight but with hardness in my voice I said, "I'm risking my life for you. I could walk away right now and let you deal with this yourself but I know you would cock it up and they would come after Heather and probably me as well. So, I'm going to do it but there's a price. In the scheme of things, it's a bargain."

I could see him weighing his options. Regardless of anything else about him, he knew when he had no choice. He nodded.

I got off the bar stool, walked out and went back to the apartment to set the plan in motion.

FIFTY-TWO

I laid low for the rest of the day. Watched a Netflix documentary on the National Lampoon and two episodes of a food show with David Chang, one about pizza and one on fried chicken. It made me hungry so I ordered sushi delivered from Sushi on Chapel. They don't really have delivery but if it's not busy, they'll run something over. They also stock Mexican coke so I splurged and got two bottles. It went perfectly with a Spider Roll.

Around 10:00, Reilly called to check in. I told him about the meeting with Hugh and that I would be making the swap tomorrow. We talked for a short while but I could tell he was tired so I said I needed to sleep. He gave me a ration of shit for being old but he knew I was doing it for him. I hung up and drank the other coke. Nothing like pure cane sugar at bedtime for a sound sleep. I took a couple of Tylenol PMs and went to bed.

I awoke the next morning to my burner phone ringing. I'd left it on the table next to the bed in case.

It was Barton. I had a feeling he would call early. I groggily said hello.

"Shore, got our money?" Almost yelling. I tried to shake off the drugs and answer.

"Barton. Nice to hear from you. How's things?"

I could swear I heard a growl.

"Always with the jokes. I'll repeat, do you have our money?"

He said it slow, enunciating each word, like he was talking to someone not quite all there. I answered in the same cadence.

"Not. Yet. But. Soon."

I wanted him pissed off, wanting to do me harm. Pliable.

I went on, "I'll have a location and a time later this morning. I'll call you. Use this number?"

He paused then said yes. The timing of this had to be spot on.

I hung up.

It took me a while to get out of bed but I finally did and went to the kitchen to put up some coffee. My regular phone rang. It was White Clarence.

"Yo, Shore, got my money?"

There seemed to be a pattern developing. I sighed.

"I should have it all by noon. I was going to call you and arrange a meet. I'll come there. I have a place that'll be safe and where I'll feel safe, away from the street."

No answer. Finally, "Okay. How much product do they want?"

This was new to me. I asked him, "What will four thousand buy?"

He chuckled. "Weird number. About 3 pounds, give or take, but it is very high-quality weed. They can cut that down, divvy it up and double their money. You thinkin' about some for yourself?"

My turn to laugh. "Nah, I like to relax the liquid way."

I had enough of the friendly chit-chat. "So, I will call you back on this number in a hour or so and give you where and when details." And hung up.

Parts 3 & 4 in place. Waiting on the FBI.

I tried Dillard's number again. He picked up immediately.

"Shore, I was going to call you. We're interested in being there for your party. Where and when?"

I weighed how much he would let me get away with. I tried to bluff.

"I'm still waiting on details. I'll call you within the hour, okay?"

He didn't answer immediately. I waited thirty seconds. "Dillard?"

I could hear paper shuffling and muffled voices. He finally came back on and said okay. I hung up from him and tried to steady myself.

All the pieces were in place on the board. I just needed to avoid checkmate.

FIFTY-THREE

I got dressed in loose fitting clothes, loose enough to hide the gun. I grabbed my regular phone and the burner phone and left the apartment. I went through the backway and across to the lot and walked up three flights of stairs to the rental car. I had a few errands to run before I put this into play. I drove over to the 91/95 connector and got on 91 going north towards Hartford. I got off at Exit 9 and made my way over to the Target store there.

Once in Target, I headed to the Housewares department, where I found four industrial-sized flashlights. I went over to the tool section and found a bolt cutter. Just in case.

I got back on the highway towards NY, merging onto 95 and past Long Wharf on one side and the harbor on the other. It was a beautiful day. I took it until the Saw Mill exit and pulled off into the Starbucks parking lot. I went in and got an Americano, with the new Blond expresso. Supposed to be smoother. Wasn't sure how much smoother it was but it made for a mighty fine cup of coffee.

I sat in the car and began to dial. I decided to bring the players in according to furthest distance. I called Barton on the burner and told him the address of the factory and that the swap would be happening around 1:00. That he should come in a car so that they could keep a lower profile. He was his usual charming self and said they would be there then hung up on me.

I called Macklin and Pete next, gave them the same where and when information but told them the deal was going down at 12:30. Macklin actually said "10-4" before he hung up.

I called Dillard. He had questions. How many? Where exactly? Were there places they could set up reconnaissance teams? Did I think a sniper was necessary?

I told him he worried too much and gave him the particulars and that he should be there at 12:45, covertly. That I thought the bikers would be coming in a car to keep a low profile. I didn't think Barton would come alone but I didn't think he'd bring an army either. I was pretty sure he thought I was an easy mark so I was betting on four Druids in the car.

I sat and sipped my coffee. At around 11, I called White Clarence. A flunky picked up and told me he was "in disposal, which means he's in the can." I closed my eyes and asked him to have Clarence call me on this number. Ten minutes later, the burner phone rang.

"Yo, Tommy Shore. Ready to do some wheelin' and dealin'?"

This couldn't be over soon enough.

"Yes I am. Are you?"

A pause.

"I am, I am. But I was thinking you should come here, to my crib."

I was prepared for this. I waited a minute to make him think I was considering it. Then spoke, in a hard monotone.

"Look, I'm doing this because it's my job. I have no skin in this game. I can walk away. You can come after the two of them and you can come after me. But you're a businessman so you'll understand that, if I'm going to do this, it's gonna be on my terms, where I feel safe. There's an abandoned factory a friend of mine owned. It's private and secluded but I'll be watching it. I'm gonna come alone. I would prefer you do the same. If I see that you don't, I may bolt."

I let it sink in. He wasn't saying anything, just listening.

"Now, I have $14,000 for you. Ten goes towards what Heather owed you plus some vig, four is to purchase three pounds of weed for her business. She sells that and she's back for more.

Are we good?"

He paused again, then finally said okay.

I breathed out, trying not to let him hear me doing that. "Okay, I'll give you the address and we can meet at noon."

I gave him the information and hung up. I had 45 minutes to set this up and hope that everyone followed directions. If I was a bookie, I would be taking heavy odds against myself.

I drove down to the center of Allingtown, then up the dead-end street that the factory was at the end of. I went around to the back and drove straight to the third bay. I took the four monster flashlights out of the trunk and walked up the cement stairway, putting them on the landing. I could see no one had come back here since I had first scouted it out. I didn't need the bolt cutter.

I put everything behind it and kicked open the door. One of the glass panes shattered as it popped open and hit a stack of pallets too close behind it.

I gathered the flashlights and turned one on. It was as I had seen through the window, with stacks of wooden pallets everywhere. I was glad to see that there was much more light coming through the windows that I had first thought. I found a clearing surrounded by pallet stacks and moved a few to hold the three remaining flashlights. I set up the lights in a way that I could stand in the shadows of the crisscrossing beams. And kept one close as I waited for White Clarence to get here.

He arrived ten minutes later. As expected, he had two of his guys with him, the two that he sent to the Owl to keep an eye on me. I could see the roof of the SUV through one of the windows and saw that he had left one guy hanging back to keep watch, to stay with the vehicle.

Clarence came waddling through the door first, and waited for his eyes to adjust to the darkness. He was nervous and motioned for the other two to follow him in. He yelled out for me.

"Yo, Shore, you here?"

I turned on the flashlight in my hand and stepped out from behind the pallet stack. I had placed the bag of cash between the opening where the forklift would go. I left it there.

"Here." I shined the light towards the ceiling, keeping their vision of me off balance.

Clarence used the side of his hand to shield his eyes but I noticed he kept his right hand in his sweat jacket pocket.

"What's up, Dawg? Why the light show? Let's just do this thing and go home. You got the cash?"

I smiled. "I do. Where's the weed?"

The bigger one of his sidekicks stepped forward and laid a small box down on the floor. He used his foot to kick it closer to me. I crouched down and picked up the package inside. I had no idea what I was looking for but it felt like the weight was right and it had that smell that occasionally wafted through the Owl as it got later in the evening.

"Seems right." I used my foot to push it back towards where the money was but Clarence stopped me.

"Whoa, bro. Not so fast. I need to see the cash." He was pointing at me with his hand still in his pocket, making it clear that he was packing.

I needed to stall. "Understood. It's here. I have it in a bag. I'm going to reach in back of this stack of pallets and get it, then throw it to you. Good?"

He nodded but I could see the sidekicks positioning themselves for possible gunplay. I stalked some more. "Easy, fellas. I'm not about to take on the three of you by myself. I'll get the bag."

As I went for the bag, I heard a noise and when I looked back, Barton and three Druids had come in the door. I saw Barton use a bat to take out the smaller sidekick while the other two beat the bigger one and the fourth one held a gun on Clarence.

I heard Barton call my name, straight out of The Warriors. "Shore, come out and play!," then laugh.

I stepped out from behind the stack. "You're early."

He laughed again. "Yeah, well, I figured we'd be better off showing up before the cops came. Right? You got cops on the way here?"

Clarence turned to glare at me. He was piecing it together. "You're a dead man, Shore. I'm gonna find you after this and put a bullet in you."

I could see movement in the doorway as he was talking.

I moved back behind the stack as Macklin and Pete came through the door, guns drawn. As Pete yelled "Freeze," the two Druids turned with their guns drawn and one went off. I saw Macklin use his pistol on the side of the head of the one nearest the door while Pete shot the other one in the leg. The one that had been holding the gun on Clarence fired and I saw the big man go down, a pool of blood forming around his head. Pete turned and shot him through the heart.

I felt the liquid running down my arm before I felt the throb. I looked down and realized I had been shot by the Druid who fired when the DEA guys came in. I sat down on a small stack of pallets and gripped my arm, trying to keep pressure on it.

Barton had taken advantage of the chaos and bolted out the door, but Dillard was waiting for him, along with six other Feds. Barton made the mistake of pulling on them and they put him down immediately.

I heard Macklin yelling at me. "Shore, are you okay?" My head had started to throb and I felt dizzy. It took all I had to get up and show myself. "I've been hit but I'm okay." I used my foot to push the box of pot towards them. I had ticked the bag in my loose pants and left the gun in its place. "Here's the weed."

Macklin came over and helped me out the door and down the stairs. He yelled to Pete that I needed to go to the ER. Dillard came over immediately. "I'll take him." Macklin started to protest but Dillard flashed his FBI badge and he backed down. I was loaded into one of the Fed cars and taken to the Yale-New Haven ER. The last thing I remembered was the face of the nurse that had been at the Owl with Rosalind on the night we met.

FIFTY-FOUR

I woke up in a hospital bed two days later. There was
an IV attached to my right arm and my left wrist was
restrained by leather straps attached to the side railing.

I looked around the room. There was another bed
with a young black kid in it. He was maybe 10 years old
and had been staring at me. He seemed happy I was
awake.

"Yo, Mister. You're alive! I thought you was dead.
We all did."

I looked at him. "Who's we?" It was hard to talk and
my voice was raspy. I needed water. I tried to pour some
from the pitcher on the table next to the bed but the
strap made it difficult. The kid got out of bed and came
over, took the pitcher from my hand and poured some
water into a blue plastic cup and handed it to me. I
whispered my thanks then laid back and closed my eyes
again.

I woke up an hour later. A young woman was
sitting with the boy and they were both looking at me.

She got up and walked over. She was very pretty, maybe 30.

She straightened out my blankets and asked me if I was hungry. I shook my head no.

"Well, you should eat something. Especially if they're weaning you off morphine." She nodded at the IV drip.

I looked over at it. Explained why I felt like I was encased in velvet.

I looked back at her. "Are you a nurse?"

She smiled. "Why, I couldn't be a doctor?" Teasing.

I smiled back. "No, too good of a bedside manner, not enough arrogance. By the way, you've got a good kid there."

She beamed. "His name is Richard. He just had his appendix out. Shouldn't be getting out of bed, though."

She feigned annoyance. He chuckled then hid under the covers.

"That's my fault. He was helping me get a drink of water. My mouth was very dry."

She laughed. "That's the drugs, too. I'll get the floor nurse," and walked out the door. I looked at the kid and winked. I tried to give him a thumbs up with my left hand but the strap cut into my skin.

His mother came back in and a few seconds later, the nurse that I remembered from that night I met Rosalind followed her. She looked at me and asked how I felt. She had a great voice, husky and sexy, like Brenda Vaccaro in her heyday. I told her I was fine but had a nasty headache. She said that was the slow weaning off the drugs and that my arm might start hurting where I'd been shot. That the bullet had clipped an artery and that I'd lost a lot of blood.

I nodded at it all but my concentration was not there. I was falling asleep again when she leaned down and whispered in my ear, "I wrapped the bag up with your clothes, put it in a plastic bag and locked it in the closet. All good."

I smiled at her then fell fast asleep.

When I awoke, it was dark out.

FIFTY-FIVE

On day three, Dillard came to my room and removed the cuffs. I was alert, almost fully weaned off the morphine. The pain in my arm was ridiculous. I tried to misdirect my thoughts.

"Dillard! G-man to the rescue. How goes the battle for truth, justice and the American way?"

He gave me a tolerant smile. "Hurts, doesn't it?"

I asked if he'd ever been shot and he nodded that he had but the conversation ended there.

I asked if him if I was under arrest. He shook his head. "No, the strap was for your protection. You were thrashing around those first few days. They had to tie you down so you wouldn't pull out the IV."

He paused. "On the other hand, you may get a citation for criminal trespass on private property."

I let the little joke sink in and then asked him what the final damages were. He looked at me and I finally saw him smile. "You're a very lucky man, Shore. White Clarence is dead and his guys are in bad shape. One had his head smashed in with a bat and will eat from a straw for the rest of his life. The other two will do time. Barton and one other Druid are dead. The other two have decided to turn state's witness and will go into a program. I seriously doubt that there will be retaliation from Druids. Word was Barton had gone rogue and was acting without the sanction of the head guys."

I let some breath out slowly. I was a lucky man. I asked him about Macklin and Pete, the DEA guys. Dillard told me he'd given them credit as key players in the operation and had written both a letter of commendation. And they had the weed. Not a lot of weed but enough to exaggerate and make themselves heroes for a day or two.

We chatted a little more and after a while he left. He turned out to be cool. He never asked me about the money and he never asked me about the gun, which I'm sure they'd found.

I was discharged that afternoon. A different nurse came in and did the paperwork with me and fitted me with an arm sling. She unlocked my closet and pulled a curtain around my side of the room so I could have some privacy. It took me a few minutes to get my sea legs back but I finally made it out of bed and got dressed. The bag was right where Rosalind's nurse friend said it would be.

I said goodbye to Richard and his mom and thanked them for their kindness. Then I left the room, took the elevator to the first floor and walked out of the hospital.

FIFTY-SIX

I took an Uber back to my apartment. There was a pile of mail stacked neatly on the little table inside my front door. Reilly.

I called him first. He answered on the third ring.

"Yo, if it ain't Hack Reacher. Just get out? Got any good drugs?"

It felt good to hear his voice, especially sounding upbeat. "Like you give a shit. Why didn't you come see me?"

He lowered his voice. "We came, those first two days. Me and Kathy. Not sure you were gonna make it. But you're a tough one, ain't ya? After that, it was like Grand Central Station in there. I decided to wait until we could get together at the Owl. Man, it's good to talk to you. You had us worried."

I said I was sorry, that I didn't mean to make them worry. He laughed. We made a plan to meet at the Owl in an hour.

I picked up my messages. Almost all were from Hugh, first asking me to call him and then later apologizing. He must have heard what happened from Reilly. I called Heather but Hugh answered.

"Tommy. Thanks for calling back. We heard what happened. Are you okay?"

I didn't really want to talk to him but I needed to play it out. "Yeah, I'm fine. A lot of pain but the doctors say I'm lucky, that I'll keep the arm."

There was silence on the other end. Finally, "So, Clarence is dead. We don't have to deal with that rat bastard anymore, eh?"

I bristled. "There's no 'we' in this, Hugh. I'm done. The weed and the money were confiscated by the DEA. I've been warned not to get involved with these kinds of people again and I'm gonna heed that warning."

Silence again. Until he said, "Well, easy come, easy go. I still have the $5K so I'm ahead of the game. I need it, though. Got a new project I'm looking to invest in, where..."

I hung up. He was making me tired.

I cleaned myself up a bit and then went across the street to the Owl. Reilly was already waiting.

I sat down next to him and slid a paper bag over to him. He looked inside at the 8 packets of ten 100-dollar bills, clipped together. And for the first time since we'd been friends, he was speechless. I laughed at the look on his face.

"Consider Hugh's debt paid up...just don't ever mention it to him, okay? Now, what are we drinkin'?"

Callie came over as I said that with a tray of six shots. We downed the first one, toasted "Up the Queen" and "Slainte", then downed the next ones. We were just getting started.

EPILOGUE

"Jeez, Tommy, whatcha do, inhale that burger?"

I looked at Meredith and smiled. It was good to have my appetite back.

"That is a mighty tasty burger, Mer, mighty tasty."

She laughed and started to take my plate. I grabbed the last remaining fries. "Good to the last drop." She kept laughing as she shook her head and walked away.

I was in a great mood. My arm was healing nicely. I'd bought a fancy black sling, at first to match my jacket, but now I was using it everywhere. A great conversation starter. The doctors at the clinic I'd been going to said that it could come off soon.

I'd read in the paper the version the DEA had spun about what had gone down. It was a small article. The reporter quoted both Macklin and Pete but only mentioned Dillard as a "high ranking FBI agent." I got no mention at all. They also claimed they had gotten 500 pounds of pot off the street. I agreed that it sounded a lot better than three.

A couple of days after I had walked out of the

hospital, I'd gotten a call from Heather. She was pretty low-key on the phone and my thought was that she wasn't going to be with Hugh for very much longer. She told me she was pregnant. I also got the feeling that Hugh might not be the father but didn't ask. We chatted for a few minutes and then she whispered into the phone, "Thank you." Corny as it sounds, it made me feel that it had all been worth it. White knight syndrome, I guess.

I was less melancholy the further away from the case I got. I had Rosalind's party coming up and was thinking about maybe traveling out west.

I was enjoying myself, looking forward to whatever the days may bring.

A LOOK AT BOOK TWO:
FOR A DANCER

Excelling in the private eye business, Tommy Shore no longer misses his failed publishing career. So, when he's approached by an exotic dancer at a local strip club who says she's being stalked by a mysterious assailant and wants Tommy to investigate, he doesn't hesitate.

But the stakes are higher and more deadly than they seem, for—unbeknownst to Tommy—serious mob connections are involved.

Will Tommy make it to the end of this investigation's shattering conclusion?

Part noir, part throwback, part travelogue to one of the great small cities, For a Dancer is book two in the Tommy Shore Mystery series.

AVAILABLE AUGUST 2022

ABOUT THE AUTHOR

Lawrence Dorfman has more than thirty years of experience in the bookselling world, including stints at Simon and Schuster, Penguin, and Harry N. Abrams. He is the author of the bestselling Snark Handbook series including *The Snark Handbook: Politics and Government Edition*, *The Snark Handbook: Insult Edition*; *The Snark Handbook: Sex Edition*, *Snark! The Herald Angels Sing*, and *The Snark Handbook: Clichés Edition*. He lives in Hamden, CT with his wife.